// True Heart

SARAH STAPLEY

QUEST FOR A
True Heart

SARAH STAPLEY

WestBow
PRESS
A DIVISION OF THOMAS NELSON
& ZONDERVAN

Copyright © 2014 Sarah Stapley.

All rights reserved. No part of this book may be used or reproduced by any means, graphic, electronic, or mechanical, including photocopying, recording, taping or by any information storage retrieval system without the written permission of the publisher except in the case of brief quotations embodied in critical articles and reviews.

WestBow Press books may be ordered through booksellers or by contacting:

WestBow Press
A Division of Thomas Nelson & Zondervan
1663 Liberty Drive
Bloomington, IN 47403
www.westbowpress.com
1 (866) 928-1240

Because of the dynamic nature of the Internet, any web addresses or links contained in this book may have changed since publication and may no longer be valid. The views expressed in this work are solely those of the author and do not necessarily reflect the views of the publisher, and the publisher hereby disclaims any responsibility for them.

Any people depicted in stock imagery provided by Thinkstock are models, and such images are being used for illustrative purposes only. Certain stock imagery © Thinkstock.

ISBN: 978-1-4908-5052-8 (sc)
ISBN: 978-1-4908-5053-5 (e)

Library of Congress Control Number: 2014915894

Printed in the United States of America.

WestBow Press rev. date: 10/08/2014

My mother was intrigued by a thought from Luke 19:12-26. She began to wonder what it would be like to live in the Millennium. She shared her thoughts with me and said she would like to read a book about it. For her inspiration and godly living, as well as my father's example, this book has become a reality, in hopes that we too would press on for the prize of the upward call[1].

Continue to serve. Thanks for always being so encouraging,
SStapley

Chapter 1

Timothy[2] carefully smoothed the dirt around his tomato plants, removing the final evidence of animal visitors. "Ahh, that's better," he whispered to himself.

He was very particular when it came to the appearance of *his* garden, or rather his family's garden. He knew animals nibbled on the plants, he didn't mind, there was plenty, but he preferred to pretend that there was nothing else around, it was just him and his garden, together, his sacred place.

He methodically turned his head viewing the rows of brightly colored vegetables and the verdant fields beyond. His 5' 9" frame shuddered as he let out a heavy sigh. His deep, brown eyes surveyed his fields. There was something so captivating about plants, how from little seeds they could spring into such various entities, producing a wide variety of edible products and a vast array of amazing green leaves. To him it was like watching a baby, utterly captivating.

In the distance he could see the canopy of trees spreading over the land, it was the great African forest, it surrounded their territory's clearing. The tall trees made a distinct dividing line between the busy earth and the vacant, vast blue sky. But, as much as he loved the plants, his mind was not on them, no his thoughts were reeling from yesterday's revelation.

"I can't believe I won't be here for the harvest," he uttered in frustration as he banged his hoe down into the earth, his normally smooth brow furrowed. In his entire life he had never missed a harvest; he was always a part of every action and for the past few years every decision.

His tan forehead rested on his hands which clung to the end of his trusty hoe, causing his brown hair to fall across his anxious forehead. "What am I going to do?" he mumbled as he shrugged.

Really, he had no choice, it was law; the eldest son must go and represent the family. To disagree or disobey would be unheard of, no one would ever think of doing that, besides the consequences for not going…. Timothy's stomach lurched, his heart pained and he felt ill. It wasn't an option. He would have to go, he would take his father's place, he would make the journey. He felt like throwing up. The sigh Timothy let out came from deep down; his family would harvest *his* crops, he would NOT.

"Every year the head representative of the family journeys to Jerusalem for the Feast of Booths. It has always been my father's responsibility," Timothy moaned as he picked up his hoe and walked to another patch of disturbed earth. "Why did I have to be the eldest and the new head of the Steade family? My father can go and represent the family for the Feast of Tabernacles! But, no! Not this year! This year I have to go!" Timothy came down hard with the hoe, nearly clipping one of his beloved tomato plants. He paused, trying to gain his composure.

As the eldest son, an unmarried man and dedicated worker of the fields, it was, as he was told, now his turn to represent the Steade family in Jerusalem. He was to be there on the 15th day of Tishri[3], mere weeks away. "Why?! Why should I have to make this journey!? My father has always done it and his father before him! Why does it have to be my turn now!?" Timothy looked up in the sky, too afraid to say the words out loud, but he let them pour from his heart anyway. He had to be the one to offer a lamb this year before the "LORD of hosts[4]", the "Son of the Most High[5]". It would be him and no one else.

He trembled as he thought about what that would entail. The fear of the LORD made his body shudder. He knew God knew his thoughts and his feelings[6]. "How can I, a mere man, a lover of plants, stand accepted before the great and perfect God, the Lord, the king of Heaven and earth? How can I take the place of my father, a man after God's heart who walks and talks daily with God?" The turmoil in his stomach continued.

Timothy knew that during the day no words parted from his lips concerning the Lord. Timothy could not compare with his father or grandfather. Instead, he was consumed with his plants, the dirt and the great outdoors. What did he know about the Lord and what would be expected of him? Of course, he had heard his father often speak of what was required of him and how his journeys to Jerusalem went, but that didn't mean that he could now take full responsibility, at least, not at this time in his life. "What am I going to do?" he pleaded as he stared over his fields, the event's from last night appearing before him.

He could see his joyous father, Hezekiah, sitting at his desk in his study. He called to Timothy to come speak with him. His face always radiated joy and peace, actually, most of the elder generation's faces did, but last night there was an extra bit of excitement or joy, a brightness in his father's eyes that Timothy hadn't seen before.

His father was always talking about how great the LORD is and how He now reigned in Jerusalem and that everyone should offer praise and thanksgiving to Him.[7] It was as much a part of him as breathing. So it was no surprise to Timothy that his father started up a conversation about the soon coming Feast of Tabernacles.

There he sat, facing his dad across the desk, looking into the eyes of the man who had been a leader and example to him all of his life. It was because of his hard work and love of the land that Timothy had grown to love the fields so much. His dad had poured life into him as they worked the fields together. That was his education. He learned the seasons, the stars, and how to care for each type of plant. He learned his sums by multiplying the rows and crops, calculating what they would bring in, how much to store, how much they could harvest in a day. He learned of God, He who is faithful and true[8], how He always provided for them[9]. How He sent the rain and gave them bountiful crops[10]. He learned how each plant was created unique and different to bring God glory and to give everyone variety. He learned of the uses for plants and herbs and when and how to best harvest and store them. This man had taught him nearly everything he knew.

The image became like a nightmare to Timothy, except he didn't really know what a nightmare was, he had never had one. Evil, didn't exist like it used to. He thought he remembered his great grandmother saying something about visions in the night that made you uncomfortable and made it hard to sleep. "Well," Timothy thought, "this could qualify."

He could see his father's face again, as he repeated the words from last night. He could not believe what he was hearing.

"Timothy, I'm so excited. This year you are going to represent our family in City of Truth, in Jerusalem. You will leave shortly for your journey to the Holy Mountain[11]. I know you will enjoy this journey, it is amazing. God will be with you as you travel. I pray that you will draw ever closer to Him."

Timothy's jaw nearly dropped. He could still feel it pulling down. His father was not old, he was only 135[12] or so, there was no reason for him to pass this responsibility on to him now.

"I have been talking with Ross. It is known that people are stepping away from serving God. It may not be as much as it was in your great-grandfather's time, but it is happening. I want to do my part to help people serve God. Ross is going to take me to a land far from here where I can serve God in this way."

Why did he have this idea that he needed to show others about the true God and His attributes and not stay home? There would be plenty of time for him to do that, in the future! Not now! And what about him, Timothy? A shiver ran down his spine. He wondered if his father knew that he was one of the people he was talking about. One who didn't truly realize the full greatness of God, one who was walking away from Him.

Although Timothy wouldn't audibly admit it, he knew it was true. God was not his passion. He was not his first priority.

"Why don't we travel together?" Timothy thought, but he knew what his father's response would be. His mind was made up.

"You will start the journey alone, but don't worry, you'll be joined by so many people; you won't feel alone." His father continued to ramble on. Timothy couldn't understand it. His father loved this journey; he looked forward to it all year. He was always praising God and giving thanks for the many blessings that were bestowed upon him and his family. Why would his father think of not going? Why would his father say he was not going?

Timothy wondered if his father was ill. You know, slightly off his thinking. He wondered if something had happened recently that would cause his father to make such a decision. He could think of nothing. Besides, illness was practically unheard of. No one was sick[13], at least never with the sicknesses his great grandfather described from the life before the LORD began his reign on earth. So no, that couldn't be it. And death – why - that was unthinkable, death was practically unheard of too. Why, in Timothy's 85 years he couldn't remember one person in their area ever dying. He had heard of someone in a faraway country who had died, but that was because of, well, he didn't really know, they really didn't talk about it much. It was an accursed thing to die young, you knew that person must not have heard of the LORD[14], but that was not his father. His father was a man after God's own heart. He lived and breathed His LORD. With each breath and in each statement he would proclaim the greatness of God Most High. So, why this conversation? Why this change of mind? Why wasn't he going to go? It was so right for his father to go!

Timothy sighed again. Lowering his gaze from the horizon he stared at the rows of plants closest to him. The words rang through his mind again, "You will leave shortly. I know you will enjoy this journey, it is amazing!" He knew this day would eventually come. He just hoped it wouldn't be this soon.

He wasn't particularly worried about the journey, it was an extremely long distance away, but there would be multitudes of other pilgrims taking this same journey. His father had often told him of the people whom he had met along the way. How their generosity had gotten him to Jerusalem and how new friendships had been formed. He had also explained how God's character had been revealed through these people (their kindness, compassion, generosity…). Neither was he concerned about the supplies, the family planned and saved all year in preparation for the journey his father took to Jerusalem. Well, really, for the other pilgrims who journeyed, because they were always helping those who were passing by, offering food, giving them a room or bedding for the night, or sometimes just sharing an encouraging word as they passed by on their journey to Jerusalem where the throne of the LORD awaited[15] them. He was sure other families would do the same for him as he and his family had done. His father had told him of many people who had provided for him. It wasn't like he knew who they were. He guessed that he would just have to stumble upon them along the way.

Timothy gazed back up at the horizon, this time looking far beyond what he could physically see. He imagined the path he would take and he tried to imagine the place it would lead him. He knew he should be excited, his father had always come home so elated, ecstatic – filled with praise and giving glory to the Son of the Most High who reigned with glory, honor, and truth. But the truth was, a truth he could never reveal to the rest of his family, that he wasn't excited at all. He wasn't even remotely prepared for this journey. To be perfectly honest, his heart was not in it. "What could possibly be so great beyond what is already here? This place is perfect. The vegetation, the soil, my life. Why would I want to leave? How do I know that Jerusalem is going to be worth the journey?" Thoughts continued to tumble through Timothy's mind. "Yeah, sure. God has a great deal to do with the prosperity of my crops, but in reality, I do all the work. I put in the hours of labor. I make sure they're adequately watered and given any needed supplements. I rotate the crops, spread out the compost and make sure the soil is healthy so that I grow amazingly abundant plants." He grunted in frustration, "And I need to be here to harvest them!" He picked up the hoe again, losing any sight or vision he may have had of the faraway city. He walked down another row smoothing out the ground, removing the traces of animal prints. Making it look flat and calm, far from the emotions he suppressed within him.

Sure, his father had gone each year, it was required. It wasn't as if he wasn't grateful to the LORD who reigned from the holy city of Jerusalem, because he was. He loved living in a universally peaceful, prosperous society with prevailing righteousness and longevity[16]. He loved being close to his neighbors and helping out whenever possible. He loved getting lost in his fields and nurturing each plant. He loved hearing of stories from days gone by. His great grandfather would occasionally share what life was like before the LORD returned and reigned on the earth; oh so terrible, Timothy couldn't even imagine it. He didn't want to, besides it always gave him goosebumps to hear his great grandfather's voice as he gave praise to God and how grateful he was for the change He had brought to earth. It was as if his great grandfather would literally light up as he spoke about the Messiah coming to earth through the clouds with His angels and the other saints. The picture he painted was incredible. But somehow, it didn't move Timothy, not like being in the fields did.

Timothy knew he owed God so much and he should be overjoyed at now being able to take this pilgrimage and see the holy city where the LORD reigned with truth and justice.[17] And better still, to see the LORD Himself and to offer a sacrifice of thanksgiving on behalf of him and his entire family. But he just couldn't get excited about it. Why should he when his dad could do it?

He slowly turned his tool in his hands. He finished smoothing out the end of the row. He loved his work in the fields. Nothing gave him greater pleasure than being outdoors. The smell of the dirt, the freshness in the air, the dew on the ground, the insects busily buzzing around aiding in the growing process, the way everything brightened up the earth, almost as if they themselves sang praises to God each day as the SON shone[18]. It was as if they faced their leaves to the SON, as if the LORD was walking up to meet them and they turned toward Him and grew with everything that was in them. (Well, that is what his dad had said. Timothy just knew they were mesmerizing.) Some mornings when there was dew on the leaves, the sun shone off of them and it looked as if individual golden rainbows were beaming from them, why it could light up the air and astonish a person. "Ah," smiled Timothy, "There's nothing better, no greater love than being outdoors and taking care of my garden."

His favorite place in the garden was amongst the serene fruit trees. Timothy's feet were propelled automatically in that direction, as if searching for calmness. There were a variety of trees, from banana to orange, to lemon and cocoa trees, to cotton and others. They were planted in rows together, a few of each variety. It created a sort of alcove in which he felt protected, safe and secure. It also felt secluded, cutting off the outside world (and family) and leaving him alone in his own Garden of Eden. He loved trimming, inspecting, or sitting and thinking under the trees. There was no better place on their land, or on earth as far as Timothy was concerned. At least, that's how *he* felt.

"You know, maybe it wouldn't be so bad if I didn't have to miss the harvest. Why does the Feast of Tabernacles have to come at that time?" he mumbled as he continued walking. It wasn't as if he would miss all of it, but he would miss most of it. He was sure to see others bringing in their harvest as he travelled. His father told him there were plenty of farms lining the roads all the way to Jerusalem. Each family had sufficient land to grow a variety of fruits and vegetables to sustain their entire family[19] as well as have some extra to spare if ever a person stopped by in need of nourishment (especially people on their way to Jerusalem). It was "law" of sorts, really it was one of the Messiah's attributes that was so important to follow[20] and exemplify - His care and provision for others.

"Maybe, I can stop for a day or two at some of the farms and help them work. I wonder if they would let me. Or do I have to be fully and completely, body, mind and soul set apart for the journey?" Timothy wondered. He supposed that some of the farmers might let him or at least they might share their knowledge; teach him new growing techniques or other information. Or perhaps he could gain some new type of vegetation to grow at home. They might even share some seeds with him that he could plant when he returned home. Although, somehow that didn't seem quite right, that wasn't supposed to be the purpose of his journey. He didn't let his thoughts go too far in that direction because he started to feel a tinge of guilt. The thought probably should not have even crossed his mind. It actually seemed selfish, even though it would benefit his family. Imagine, thinking more about vegetation than God. He groaned again, "This isn't a good idea, Dad." How he wished he could say it to his father, but he couldn't and he wouldn't.

Ah! He would miss his time in the fields. "It's not that I don't think my family is capable of bringing in the harvest, but…" he paused, debating if he should voice the next words, knowing that whether or not he said them, God knew what he was thinking. "I just don't want to go. It falls at the wrong time, its weeks, maybe even months away from my garden and my family." Timothy ran his fingers through his hair and held onto one of the large tree branches. He looked up into the sky, his eyes pleading with God, begging that He would change his father's mind.

"Timothy," Adam called, "Dad would like to see you. He's by the pond."

"Okay," Timothy responded as he let go of the branch and twirled the hoe around.

"Here, let me put that away for you."

"Thanks." Timothy handed it to Adam and methodically walked toward the pond. Would God answer his half-prayer half-plea?

Chapter 2

"Hi, Dad. Adam said you wanted to see me," Timothy hesitantly greeted as he approached his father by their family pond. He perched on the end of the bench facing the water and gazed out at the land beyond. The grass was lush and green in that area. The pond extended a great distance; it was more like a lake. The size was more than enough to provide water for their family as well as their plentiful livestock.[21] The sheep baaed just a short distance from them as they wandered to a shadier area under some of the fruit trees, his fruit trees. They were such docile creatures. Not a care in the world. They calmly meandered around their land munching on the grass or drinking from the pond. Occasionally a cow would wander over and graze beside the sheep. Sometimes other animals, like zebras or deer, would come and also feast on the lush grass. They were never a problem. All the animals got along well together and shared in the bounty.

It really was an amazing spot on their land. His grandfather had often told him some of the history about it.

Quest for a True Heart

"You know, this pond used to only be 1/7[h] the size it is today."

"Really," I would say and eagerly urged him to continue, "how'd it get so big then?"

"Why, my grandson, it is a direct result of God's blessing on us, for serving Him. You know God loves to care for His people. As long as we serve Him, He will bless us and our efforts. Why your great grandfather made that decision many years ago. We have gone up to Jerusalem each year to worship the King and offer a sacrifice during the Feast of Tabernacles. Your great grandfather will never forget the many changes this earth has been through. This earth used to be a terrible place. Life was so dead, everything brown and dying. Nothing was happy, nothing, not even the animals. It was a stark place to live and a dark world at that time. Everything was under terrible punishment. But then, the LORD came down from heaven and fought for this here world. His angels took charge and reclaimed the earth for God and a vast change took place. Plants began to grow well again, animals multiplied and were happier. The animals started getting along and they weren't filled with fear anymore. People changed too. Only those who served God were left and what a time of praise they had. Oh praise the LORD! The earth is full of His fullness! The earth shines with His glory[22]!"

"Yeah, Grandpa, but what does that have to do with our pond?"

"Well, the praising never stopped. So long as we praise - God will bless. And bless us he has. I've seen this pond grow over the years[23]. But you remember this, if ever that pond starts to shrink and our plants don't look so vibrant, you better take a real serious look at yourself, you hear, because it will be your praise that determines their growth and our blessing and prosperity. 'Blessed of the Lord be [this] land, with the choice things of heaven, with the dew, and from the deep lying beneath'[24]; just like Jacob's blessing to Joseph from God, so God promises to us for our land at this time."

"How do you know, Grandpa?"

"God says so. He said, 'It will be that whichever of the families of the earth does not go up to Jerusalem to worship the King, the LORD of hosts, there will be no rain on them.'[25] And when God says something He means it. No rain means devastation. No water for you, your family, the animals or the plants, all *because we are not serving God the way we should. So you keep an eye on this here pond and on those trees. Then we will know the true state of your heart."*

"Oh," I had stated.

"Do you remember the verses you learned to say each morning and night?" he asked me.

"Yeah, of course. *'And it shall come to pass if you surely listen to the commandments that I command you today to love the Lord your God and serve him with all your heart and all your soul, that I will give rain to your land, the early and the late rains, that you may gather in your grain, your wine and your oil. And I will give grass in your fields for your cattle and you will eat and you will be satisfied.*[26]"

"Nicely said, but don't just rush through it, remember this pond is a direct result of God's blessing to us. We must always show Him the respect and glory He deserves. We must worship Him and give Him praise."

As long as Timothy could remember their family was always well blessed. His relatives had always attributed it to the representative that was sent to Jerusalem to keep the feast of booths. If they did that then God kept His promise of blessing them, even though they were not descendants of Abraham.

As a gardener he knew how important this pond was. He always had excess water on hand for his projects. Plus, it looked absolutely magnificent. Whether it was really there because of his family's past and present choices, he wasn't so sure, but it was there, and that he was sure of.

His thoughts were interrupted by his father. "Timothy, you have always loved the garden, this is true, but in your gardening, have you ever taken time to consider the animals God made?"

The animals? Consider the animals? What a peculiar question. He thought for a moment, "Watch the animals? I see the effects that they leave, their footprints all over the rows in the vegetable garden, bite marks out of the fruit and some vegetables. Yeah, I notice them or at least what they do. I often see results from their feasts, but if I had a choice, I would prefer that they wouldn't be there," he thought. It wasn't like Timothy didn't appreciate animals, he did, but he preferred the bees or things that assisted with pollinating, not those that ate his hard work. So he didn't have as much appreciation for the others, those larger creatures that would trample through his garden.

He took a slow deep breath and then responded with what he thought might be an acceptable answer, "I suppose. I normally see them eating, drinking or resting. The sheep or cattle are normally around the pond. The trees nearby provide shade for them and the water gives them a cool drink as they desire." He wasn't sure what his father was getting at, but he hoped this would be a satisfactory answer.

"Yes, this is true, but have you ever really watched the animals?"

"I guess that wasn't it." Timothy thought. What was he getting at? He sure hoped he wasn't going to tell him that he now needed to care for animals and forget gardening. How devastating that would be to have to look after the creatures. Watching them grow would provide no satisfaction for him, nor would watching them eat all his crops after he had worked so hard. It would be a boring and devastating job. As far as he was concerned, they could fend for themselves, they needed no caretaker. What could one possibly want to learn from animals anyway? "No, Father, I have not sat and carefully observed the animals."

His father gave a small grunt, almost a "Humph," as he continued to look out over the livestock as they were feeding and drinking. There was what seemed to Timothy like an exceedingly long pause. It was turning into an awkward silence. Timothy felt that it must be more on his part than his fathers. Truth be told, he was starting to get antsy. What was so important that he had to come to his father? Why couldn't it have waited until they retired for the evening, after his work was done? They could have had a talk in the study again. He knew his father realized that harvest time was a busy time and there was much to do in preparation for it. It wasn't like it overwhelmed him, but he loved how it kept him busy and required even more of his time and devotion. His father would know, especially with him leaving shortly, that there were many things Timothy wished to accomplish. He wanted to do as much as he could before he began his journey. But here they were, sitting together, not talking, but just staring at the livestock, watching the sheep as they ate.

Just as Timothy turned to face his father more squarely and was about to ask him the purpose for calling him there, his father began to speak. "You are to carry a lamb with you to Jerusalem. It will be one of our new lambs, less than a year old. You must choose it carefully, for remember it is to be perfect. There is to be no spot or blemish on it[27]. You will carry it with you all the way to Zion[28] and offer it as one of your sacrifices." He was still looking over the scenery, the pond, the animals and surrounding area. He was talking as if Timothy was just a bystander, not directly related to what he was saying. As Timothy looked at him he noticed that his eyes were not really focused on the scene before him, but were imagining something else. Perhaps he was seeing Jerusalem and the sacrifices. Perhaps he was imagining what it would be like NOT to be there this year to see and offer praise to God as he had done for so many years now.

Timothy quickly glanced back out over the field and pond. His heart raced a little faster as thoughts whizzed through his mind. "How could this be? He had to take care of an animal now? This was not his specialty. How could he possibly carry the animal so many miles to Jerusalem without it getting hurt? And what if he was given special seeds or plants from others that he wanted to keep? How could he carry both? What a burden, what a hindrance! What was he to feed it? How would he get along the trail? It had to be perfect, without blemish when he got there, that meant nothing could happen to it on the way. What was he thinking! He couldn't take care of a lamb, especially not on such a journey! He couldn't do that, he was a farmer, a gardener, a lover of plants, not animals. There was no way! It would just slow his journey down even more!"

He respected his father, as he should, it was one of the many laws that came out of Jerusalem[29], and he had never had a problem with it before. 'Honor your father and your mother[30], it *had* made life so wonderful. But, to carry a lamb, all those miles to Jerusalem! He started shaking his head, ready to contradict his father's request, ready to tell him he couldn't go. He was glad his father was not paying attention to him, but seemed to be lost in thought. Timothy's own thoughts were soon interrupted by his father.

"You will be leaving first thing Yom She-Nee[31]. You are not to take anything else with you, aside from the clothes on your back[32], three days worth of food, some blankets, some money to purchase your other sacrificial animals, and the lamb that you choose. The rest will be provided for you by God's people on your journey. You will find many willing hands to assist you along the way."

"But Dad, I...I...I can't take care of a lamb. I don't know the first thing to do."

"You will carry the lamb to ensure it is not hurt. Stop often throughout the day to feed the lamb and let it walk around for exercise, but you must remember, do not let it get hurt, your lamb must be perfect. You will make it safely with the lamb and offer it as a sacrifice at the temple[33] in this you will do as the LORD of hosts requires and worship the King at the Feast of Booths[34]." His gaze seemed to drift even further from the pond. He stared out over the forest and beyond the horizon. A glow came from his face and his smile brightened and stretched from ear to ear. "Ah, yes," he continued, "you will go to Jerusalem, the city of Zion." His eyes narrowed as he pictured the sight. "Many will gather, much praise will be sung, but all you need to see is the One, the Mighty God who sits on the throne. He alone is worthy and is worth a much further journey and a much greater sacrifice.

> "Great is the LORD, and greatly to be praised,
> In the city of our God, His holy mountain.
> Beautiful in elevation, the joy of the whole earth,
> Is Mount Zion *in* the far north,
> The city of the great King.
> God, in her palaces,
> Has made Himself known as a stronghold."

His voice continued in a whisper tone. Timothy could only make out a few lines of what he was saying.

> "We have thought on Your loving-kindness, O God,
> In the midst of Your temple.... For such is God,
> Our God forever and ever;..."[35]

Sarah Stapley

As Timothy gazed over the pond and field he had a sinking feeling in his heart. What lamb? How would he know which one to select? Which one would be perfect to offer to the King? The enormity of the task began to dawn on him. It wasn't just travelling with this lamb that was going to be a problem. It was going to be offering the lamb. If he were to go, now, in his father's place, he could not offer a sacrifice worthily, as his father and grandfathers had. He did not give praise as his family did. He couldn't pretend, God would know. How was he going to get through this, or get out of it? He glanced at his father again. He sat silently now, with his face lifted heavenward. His face beamed as if it was the sun itself shining, while Timothy's heart sank deeper in misery.

Timothy tried to hide his emotions from off of his ashen face. He tried to process what he knew he would have to do. But he knew he couldn't make a choice, he didn't know what to look for. It was best to ask his father's opinion. He would deal with the major issue later. He would figure out a way. "Which lamb would you take, Dad?" he asked hesitantly, not wanting to disturb his father's reverie, but desperately in need of some direction.

His father's gaze returned to the earth as he looked around. His eyes rested near the orange trees. There were three adult sheep grazing near the foremost tree, two lambs were standing close by, grazing some and wandering some. The mother sheep would glance occasionally to check on their young and then continue their munching.

"The little one, over there, closest to its mother," he stated with the nod of his head. "Yes, that would be an excellent choice, a perfect lamb for the perfect One." Timothy's father stood, smile serene, his glowing face ever peaceful as he slowly headed toward the house. His face was still gleaming and his hands were raised. He began reciting another song, but Timothy wasn't listening. He just stared at the lamb his father had pointed out.

He was white, with little black hooves. His face was tiny and content. His little nose wiggled as he sniffed the grass and air around him. He didn't have a care in the world. He started jumping around, hopping as if he was overjoyed with something then turned back to his mother. "What am I to do? What am I thinking? I can't do this. Take care of a lamb?!? I need to go explain to Father that I'm not ready, but I can't tell him that. I don't think he'll understand.

"I need to be here with my crops. He needs to go to Jerusalem and represent the family. He is always full of praise and songs. I can't do this!" His hands pressed against his temples, his head felt like a stirred up bumblebees' nest. Questions were flying here and there, scenarios of the days ahead flashed across his mind leaving him feeling bewildered and doomed. He knew he couldn't do what his father asked, it just wouldn't work. It wouldn't be right.

Timothy looked back at the peaceful lamb, trying to calm his thoughts. With a groan he mumbled, "Well, I guess we have one thing in common little lamb." He stood up and took a few steps closer to the lamb. Kicking his feet in the grass he muttered, "We were both chosen to go to Jerusalem, both chosen to worship the King." Scuffing his feet he turned to walk toward the barn, "I hope I can survive this better than you will. If not, we're all in trouble."

Chapter 3

Ross walked down the dusty path to the main house on the Steade's property. Even though the dust kicked up around his feet, it never stayed on his radiant and exceedingly white garment,[36] it simply fell back to the ground from which it had come. He looked over the beautiful property, a haven of sorts in the vast jungle. This town had been established many, many years ago. Ross remembered when Timothy's great grandfather had journeyed here from Jerusalem. He was looking for a place to raise a family, a place of his own where he could freely praise and glorify the LORD of hosts who had rescued him from such tribulation and destruction. How grateful he was to be one of the saints that lived through those terrible times. He was even more grateful that those terrible times had ended.

Ross had been with the LORD when he returned on His white horse with His armies from heaven behind Him on their horses.[37] They came 'on the clouds of the sky with power and great glory'[38]. He and the other resurrected saints had come to rescue the saints that were still living on earth before all evil destroyed them. All it took was the word of the Lord and every man who was not a follower of God fell, as if they were slain by a sword. Their flesh was eaten by birds.[39] It was there that Ross had first met Timothy's great grandfather, Azrael. Azrael changed his name immediately after the battle to Azriel, meaning "help of God" rather than "Angel of Death."[40] He decided that every ounce of his life was going to be lived in dedication to God, he would be holy before the LORD[41].

He had done just what he set out to do. He found land far away from others. He was afraid that what had happened in the past, with evil people influencing his family, friends and even himself, might happen again. So, having married another survivor of the great battle they traveled far and built their own home in a secluded jungle, many miles southwest of Jerusalem. He named the place Aarde[42] Daal[43], meaning Land in Africa - desire to please. Azriel had planted a great vineyard with orchards and gardens.[44] He built a home for his family and he raised them to love and serve God. His children, grandchildren and great grandchildren continued to follow his example in the LORD[45]. They sang praises together and worked their land daily giving honor to the one true God. Over time others had joined him, clearing land and beginning territories of their own. That was many, many years ago.

The world had become a very different place from what it once was,[46] since the one Great Shepherd began ruling over the world[47] with justice.[48] He ruled from sea to sea.[49] There was no more fear,[50] no more evil.[51] The Great Shepherd was taking care of His children, protecting them, providing for them a world of peace as a mother would her nursing baby[52]. He had magnified Himself and made Himself known to all nations so everyone knew He was Lord[53]. He would rule forever.[54] The people who moved in around his area were also lovers of God.[55] As they began clearing land and establishing their own settlements Azriel felt no fear or concern. It was such an amazing thing to see after the terrors of the time before. Imagine- a family, a settlement, a community, whose hearts were solely sold out to God, no distractions, just service to Him. It was not something Ross ever saw when he had lived on earth many, many years before Azriel, but it was something that had been very prevalent for the past 350 years, since the LORD began His reign.

Azriel's family had remained dedicated to the LORD, going up to Jerusalem, "the city of righteousness, a faithful city"[56], each year for the Feast of Booths and daily praising God in all their work. God had bountifully blessed them because of their obedience[57] and because of their true and humble hearts[58] that desired to seek His kingdom first and His righteousness[59].

Ross considered himself very blessed to rule[60] over this territory and the Steade family. He had been put in charge of this district by the Messiah, part of his reward for the work he had done while he lived on earth[61] many years before when such evil took over the world.

He hadn't been a famous man, nor exceedingly prosperous during his lifetime. He had merely been a follower of God, realizing at a young age the importance of serving God and not chasing after material things. Sure, he had had his chance to make money. He'd been offered a full scholarship to get an accounting degree. A desk job of sorts, managing other people's money, it would have paid well, but he had turned that opportunity down to study God's precious Word. Then there was the time where he could have made it big, he had been offered a high paying job working overseas, away from his family and brothers and sisters in Christ. The stipulations were as follows, "Your work is of the utmost importance, your God, your religion, and your family will no longer have a place in your life," he was told. He had turned that job down too. Preferring to serve his God and teach his family about Him. It had not been a loss, his family had followed God and he had the opportunity to speak to many people about Christ. They too were now serving the LORD in various capacities during Christ's reign.

Ross (when he worked on earth in his earthly body) had always loved the fact that he could go to someone's job site and share what Christ had done for him. Even when he had moved away from his home country he continued to share his love for his God. Had he become prosperous? No. Famous? No, but had he changed lives? Yes, indeed he had.

Quest for a True Heart

The woman he had married had shared the same values with him. Together they raised three children, all with the same desire, to serve their God. Their simple life, in what was once known as North America, was rewarded by God at the Judgment Seat.[62] His life was as the Bible says, like a small seed, no one understood how it grew or what it was like inside, just that when it was planted, the fruits were reaped accordingly.[63] So the seed that had been sown in Ross was for God, and as the parable which Jesus told so long ago, that small seed soon grew and spread its branches and gave life to many[64] who believed, who bore fruit and became seeds that grew into more trees. That growth he did not see nor understand while he lived his life on earth, but now as he reigned with Christ over the territory that was given to him to judge,[65] he could see the many, many benefits and lives that had been touched or changed by his. He could see the countless branches added and the size of that tree that started to grow and bear fruit so many years ago when he accepted Christ.

As Ross neared the house he decided that he wanted to speak directly to Hezekiah. Since Hezekiah had just finished his conversation with Timothy at the pond the most obvious place to look for him was in his office.

"Good afternoon, Hezekiah," Ross greeted as he appeared in the study.[66] He had decided not to pass through the house and disturb the others. Since he wanted privacy he knew closing the door would keep his visit discreet.

Ross' face shone[67] like the sun and his exceedingly white garments appeared as if they were light themselves brightening up the entire room. It was as if a spot light was above him or in him, following him around, only there wasn't any light at all, but the glow could still be seen. Being in God's presence did that. Hezekiah often wondered if he could ever be close enough to God to shine[68] like Ross.

"Good afternoon, Ross."

"I see that Timothy is still outside after your discussion. Do you believe he is ready for this journey?"

"We had a brief discussion. I filled him in on some details. He is more than willing to go, I have never questioned his obedience. I am concerned that his heart is not completely ready for this. I'm not sure he truly appreciates or understands the full meaning or importance of this journey and the Feast. Nor does he understand how great God is and how different things are with the LORD reigning now then what they used to be. I also don't think he completely comprehends the impact this journey will have on all of our lives here. I am hoping that by taking a lamb with him on his journey he will learn to love it, truly love it, and he will then understand how great a sacrifice God has made for us. If he can realize this, I'm sure his heart will follow and his sacrifice will be offered whole heartedly. I'm sure he'll understand then. I am looking forward to that change in him, when he praises God for all things, not just plants. I'm looking forward to the time when he will praise God for God. When he really begins to see what an amazing Ruler we have. That will make the difference in his life."

"Yes, then this would be a good time for him to go. He does need to realize this, before he has a family." Ross smiled and raised his eyebrows at the thought. "I will watch him on his journey and join him when I need to. It is time for him to see "The Zion of the Holy One of Israel"[69] and the One who rules the earth. It is time for him to offer praise as you and your fathers before you have."

"Yes. It is time he learns the joy of the LORD, not just to be satisfied with His goodness,[70] but to stand in awe of the God of Israel[71] and to praise His name.[72] I trust that he will learn the importance of the sacrifice and fully dedicate his life to God rather than his fields. I cannot go with him, for he will then believe it is up to me to take care of the sacrifice. This is something he must do on his own, not pass on to someone else."

"I will see that he offers a worthy sacrifice and guide him as best as I can. I know this has been a tough decision for you."

Hezekiah let out a breath that he hadn't realized he was holding. What a relief, he knew God had promised to provide a shepherd to guide them through life, one who would follow God's heart and who would feed those under him with knowledge and understanding.[73] It was comforting to know that Ross would continue to be the shepherd that their family needed, whether here in Aarde Daal or on the road. Ross would be the guide to ensure that his offspring would continue to follow the Faithful One so their family would continue to receive the blessing He had promised,[74] but it was more than just a blessing, it was the realization that the LORD was the one true God who deserved all the worship, glory and praise on earth and in Heaven. It was a way of life. If only Timothy could understand that.

At that Ross disappeared[75] and showed up at the house of the next family whom he was also responsible for, to be sure that they too were sending a representative to Jerusalem for the Feast of Tabernacles.

Chapter 4

Timothy walked through the barn one last time before he would leave. His eyes wandered over his beloved tools. They had been handed down for generations, but they worked as well as if they had been newly made. He came to the pruning hooks on the wall. He hoped he would be back in time to use them to trim the trees for the next season. They did produce so much better when he pruned them. He had a knack for it, as with anything to do with plants.

He recalled the story his great grandfather had often told him about those pruning hooks as well as the plowshares.[76] He remembered watching his great grandfather carefully straighten the barn and put the tools away as he told his story.

His hand ran over the pruning hook. "You know," he said. "I once thought this thing could save my life."

"Really, Great Grandpa? What do you mean? Were you hungry? Did you think you could eat it?"

His Great Grandpa chuckled as he continued, "No, boy, I didn't need food. You see many years ago, when I was much younger, the earth was very different. There were a lot of very terrible people, people who didn't want anything to do with God; this made them very unhappy and angry. They wanted to get rid of everyone who believed in God."

"But Great Grandpa,' Timothy interjected, "there wouldn't be anyone left."

"Humph," he breathed out, "well, there were an awful lot of evil people and what seemed like so few of us who followed God. We were all gathered together in a field. They had us surrounded. Now, I had been told by a man that I trusted that God had said he would protect those who loved Him, but at that time I'm sorry to admit; I was scared. I didn't see how we could possibly win the battle. There were so few of us who had anything to protect ourselves with. You see, they were coming to kill us with whatever they could. This used to be something called a spear and the plowshares were swords."

He then bent down in the dirt and did his best to draw these "weapons" as he called them. He also tried to draw a fighting scene, but Timothy really couldn't understand it, he had never seen a battle before let alone anyone angry or frustrated, that just wasn't how people lived.

"So, what happened?"

"Just as those who had weapons who were standing on the outer circle of our group were about ready to fight, knowing that there wasn't much hope for us, the sky suddenly opened up. And there, before our eyes, in the sky was this massive white horse with a rider. His eyes were like flames from the fire and he wore many crowns. His clothes looked as if they had been dipped in blood. No one knew His name, but they called Him 'The Word of God', 'Faithful and True'.[77] Everyone stopped; our group of men and the other army. It was like everyone was frozen in their place."

"So it was the LORD that came from the sky?"

"Yes."

"The very one who sits on Jerusalem's throne now?"

"One and the same. He had a massive army behind him. They were all dressed in white and rode white horses.[78] But it wasn't His army that came down and saved us."

"It wasn't? So what happened?"

"God spoke and His fierceness was like a sword. The other army started dropping as if they had been struck. They were dying and we weren't even doing anything. It was all the Lord. Then, suddenly, as if from nowhere, yet from everywhere these birds came and ate up the dead people.[79] And what had been a terrifying scene and part of my life, disappeared into a peaceful event. The LORD destroyed all evil that day and took His rightful place on the throne in Jerusalem."

He hung up another tool. The seriousness and worry lines leaving his forehead, "We soon realized with the LORD in control we no longer needed weapons to protect or defend ourselves. We were His people and those who survived were more than willing to serve Him. So we took all of those swords and spears, ours and the enemies, and turned them into useful tools for gardening. Do you not think they have worked well for us?"

"Why yes Great Grandfather, they sure have. I can't imagine ever using them for anything different."

The reverie disappeared as Timothy inspected the last of the tools. He made sure it was in its proper place as well as well maintained for his family's use while he was gone away on his journey. These tools had served him well. He loved the feel of them in his hands, working in the yard and feeling productive.

He started to think about what might have caused such great evil and trouble in the world, but he could come to no definite conclusion seeing he had never seen such a world, so he let the thought go and made his way one last time to check on his orchards. He wanted to be sure to leave a detailed list of what to do, so that it would be done right and in the right time.

He walked through the aisle between the trees. He loved the way the branches reached out to one another, as if in greeting or caring for one another. There seemed to be a peace[80] and happiness among the plants. He couldn't really explain it, just feel it. Every tree and blade of grass was bursting full of color and life. It normally spilled over into his life, making him feel the same vibrancy. It gave him joy and hope and purpose.

His walk took him back to the pond where he decided to sit on the bench for awhile. He wasn't quite ready to go into the house. His mind was full of thoughts, reviewing all that had been discussed over the last two days and all that he hadn't dared to discuss. As he sat there he remembered a psalm his grandfather had taught him.

> "The LORD is my shepherd, I shall not want.
> He makes me lie down in green pastures;
> He leads me beside quiet waters.
> He restores my soul; he guides me in the paths
> of righteousness for His name's sake.
> Even though I walk through the valley of the shadow of death,
> I fear no evil, for You are with me;
> Your rod and your staff, they comfort me.
> You prepare a table before me in the presence of my enemies;
> You have anointed my head with oil;
> My cup overflows.
> Surely goodness and lovingkindness will
> follow me all the days of my life,
> And I will dwell in the house of the LORD forever.[81]"

Yes, he sort of understood a little about shepherds. Ross's title was a shepherd.[82] He was supposed to watch over the families in their territory. He wasn't present all of the time, but he would show up now and then to check on his family. Timothy had supposed that it was like his brother, who occasionally went to check on the sheep making sure they were satisfied, safe, and had plenty to eat. There really wasn't much danger, so it wasn't as if the sheep needed constant tending, nor did the people.

Timothy remembered his brother discussing with his father that God was like the Chief Shepherd[83] that would watch over His flock, His people. He guessed that was right because he knew he had been given many green pastures and blessings from God as well as other families in the area (at least that is where his father and grandparents said it came from). He wasn't too sure about the valley of death and comforting with a staff, or anything about enemies, but then again, he had never lived in a time where such things existed. And since he had always benefited from his family's blessings, he had never known anything else. He figured everyone had the same, land, food, and everything. Everyone in his jurisdiction followed God's laws and lived by His standards. Each one of them sent a representative to Jerusalem each year and each one in return was blessed. He figured that is what must be meant by 'My cup overflows'. He also knew that goodness and lovingkindness were from God and that they were also prominent character traits in his area. But wasn't that natural? Would it really be different if God weren't in charge; or if a person didn't go to Jerusalem? Timothy wondered if it would.

"Well, I guess it will be my turn to be 'the shepherd' and to see if I can take care of you," Timothy said as the little lamb approached the bench. He jumped around a little then settled near his feet, looking up at him expectantly.

There was something different in this lamb's eyes. They were large and deep. They carried a softness and understanding. He felt as if he could get lost in those eyes. It was as if there was security and wisdom and knowledge in the very depths of the little lamb, yet there was sadness and loneliness too. Perhaps these things had been there before, but Timothy didn't remember seeing them; then again, he didn't often look too carefully into sheep's eyes. It seemed as if the lamb knew it was going on a journey with him. It trusted him. It sent a shiver running down his back.

"You have more faith than I do little lamb." He bent over and gently patted the lamb on the head as he rose and headed toward the house. He could hear him baaing as he walked away. It gave a little tug at Timothy's heart.

Two more nights and he would begin his journey. It would be best if he got all of his notes written out for his family tonight. Tomorrow would be their day to worship and then he would be off at sunrise the following morning.

Chapter 5

The morning of the 2nd day of Elul dawned the same as any other morning. The dew was on the ground. The air was warm with a touch of dampness. The orangey pink glow lined the tree tops and spread across the horizon. Today was the day. Timothy fully awoke, stretched and rolled out of bed. After straightening his room he gathered the few things that his father had permitted him to carry and headed toward the kitchen. There was no point in prolonging the inevitable. He hadn't been able to tell his father that his heart was not in this journey and that it would be a mistake to send him. He didn't want to disappoint him, nor did he really want him to know the whole truth about how unsure he really was about God and His blessings.

His mother came over with a plateful for breakfast. Her hair was tightly tied back with a vibrant kerchief, as always. A few wisps of her dark curls always seemed to pop out around her forehead and temples which accentuated her soft, caring face. She set the plate down and turned back to her task at hand, humming as she completed each task. She readied his bag of supplies and prepared breakfast for the rest of the men. It appeared that he would be eating his last meal at home alone. Perhaps that was best. The less he said the better.

Timothy managed to swallow the nutritious grains that were on his plate. He brought his dishes to the sink and gave his mother a grateful and heartfelt thank you. She returned the hug, then handed him his three day food and water supply. She smiled and turned back to her duties. There was no talking, no discussing, no I'll miss you or see you when you get back, just a silent, 'here's your bag, go.' His mother continued humming, going on as she had done for so many years. Timothy had nothing to say in return and not wanting to interrupt her humming decided to leave quietly. Besides, any protest would be absolutely out of the question and to pretend great joy over this journey just wasn't going to happen. Timothy gathered the rest of his supplies and headed for the door. He needed to get the lamb, say farewell to his dad, and be on his way. Perhaps if he focused on getting there and getting back it wouldn't be so bad or so long.

As he exited the front door he was surprised to see his father, grandfather, and great grandfather. Their bodies moved gracefully across the yard. There was extra energy and joy in each movement. It wasn't something you could emulate it was just there, a part of who they were. It had always been a part them for as long as Timothy had been alive. He noticed it more the older they got. It was in every part of them, but it was most noted in their facial expressions; their eyes were bright and their faces just seemed to glow and be uplifted as if they had just heard the greatest news and they were overjoyed. This joy radiated through their entire body. It was something that wasn't just there once in a while either. It was continual, like an extra surge of energy that consistently flowed through each of them. It was constant like a natural spring and it seemed to increase with each mention of the LORD. Even though his great grandfather was nearly 300 years older than himself and his father was well past 100, the energy and joy they carried made them seem younger and more energetic than Timothy's 85 years.

Timothy didn't understand where the joy and energy came from. He had always heard of the Lord and spoke about Him, but it did not give him the same zeal or glow. He just didn't feel that surge when he spoke of Him, like his great-grandfather, grandfather and father did. He supposed it was because he didn't really understand how the world was before the LORD reigned. Even though his father hadn't seen it either he had heard more about it from his father and grandfather before him. Another factor may have been because Timothy's interest was more in his fields. He loved growing things. That gave him joy, but it was not the same type of gushing, radiating joy that his relatives possessed when they spoke of the righteous LORD. He just didn't understand it.

"We have gathered to pray over you and bless you on your journey. We know that you are going to represent our family and we ask that you go and give glory and honor to the King as He deserves," declared his father.

"We have each had this opportunity and know what a great privilege it is. You cannot imagine such greatness until you see it. Your eyes will be opened to many things. His greatness will far exceed all you could ever think or take in during one trip. He is mighty and powerful. His name is to be praised above every name! As much as we would love to go with you, it has been decided that you will travel alone," his grandfather continued as he sang out praises to God. His face lifted to the sky, "Go and worship our King."

"God will guide your journey. Turn to Him for all of your needs," great grandfather stated, "He will never let you down."

The men circled around Timothy, put their hands on him and prayed over him. "Gracious Father and Lord of all, we are so grateful to send young Timothy as our representative to Jerusalem to offer a sacrifice to You in remembrance of the sacrifice You gave. We ask for Your guidance upon him as he travels and that you would show Yourself to him along the way. Lord, fill his heart with praise and adoration for You. Let his lips sing forth praise as he approaches Your city. Let him come before You humbly and with fear and reverence of Your greatness. Let him offer His sacrifice of thanksgiving with a true heart." His father's prayer continued on as he sang out praises to the LORD, his grandfather and great grandfather joining in with their "yes, yes" and "please Lord".

As they raised their heads from the prayer and looked up into the sky in unison they said, "Behold, this is our God for whom we have waited that He might save us. This is the LORD for whom we have waited; Let us rejoice and be glad in His salvation."[84]

With that Hezekiah placed the little lamb in Timothy's arms, gave him a side hug with a pat on the back and said, "Thus you shall act in the fear of the LORD, faithfully and with a loyal heart."[85] Then he headed inside with the other men for breakfast. As the door closed behind them Timothy realized that he was now on his own, headed to Zion, the great city of God. There was no making excuses now. Clutching onto the lamb, he took a deep breath and headed for the road.

He began his journey, heading east, with the rising sun before him. His shadow stretched behind him, lagging in the distance. He knew there would be many miles of walking before he would reach the sea. He would travel through the dense forests then out into the more open plains and hills. He had been told that they were once desert lands with nothing but dirt and sizzling heat, but that was before the LORD came to reign on earth. Since then many things had changed.

Once he arrived at the sea he would catch a passenger boat; he would work on the boat in trade for his fare. He would then arrive at the peninsula south of the great city and walk the rest of the journey with other pilgrims. This too had once been barren land, but no more. From what his father and grandfather told him it was some of the most fertile land. He was told that the crocuses that blossomed[86] would appear to be singing out to God as one approached Zion. He was interested in this, because he could not imagine land more beautiful than his home territory. Timothy was to arrive before the 15th of Tishri, for that was when the Feast began[87] and no laborious work was to be done on that day.

He did hope that this little lamb would be able to withstand the journey and that he would make it without incident. He shifted the lamb in his arms, trying to make him comfortable.

Chapter 6

Timothy felt odd leaving The Aarde Daal Territory for the first time. He wasn't just visiting and conversing with neighbors as he sometimes did on the outskirts of the Aarde Daal, but he was actually going to travel a great distance away from it. He had a strange kind of feeling in the pit of his stomach that he couldn't really describe. It wasn't fear, for although he was facing the unknown he didn't really have worries about it. He wasn't excited about his journey that was for sure. And the extra care of the lamb surely didn't please him. But deep down, he did have this feeling, this feeling of dread, a wondering if what his family had said was really true. Was his journey going to be the difference for their family's success? Would it really make a difference to their land? Was this journey just a tradition, a thing they had been doing for so many years that they merely felt they had to do it because they'd always done it, or was there some substance for what they said? Timothy wasn't sure, but he guessed it didn't matter for he hadn't been able to confront his father about not wanting to go, so now he was on his way. He had to go.

He knew people on his journey would be more than helpful, that was the way people were, not just because it was law,[88] but because the earth was filled with kind, gracious, and righteous people.[89] Everyone served the LORD, in every nation, in every kingdom;[90] he would find no one who wouldn't offer him help on his pilgrimage to Jerusalem, he just wouldn't.

He also knew that he was not completely alone, for God's Spirit would be with him, He was everywhere.[91] Timothy knew he could call on God anytime. He had been raised that way. That God wanted a relationship with him and would be willing to talk or listen wherever Timothy was during whatever Timothy was doing. The truth was that things always went so smoothly while he was working in the gardens therefore he rarely felt the need to call out to God or talk with Him. He did pray when his family was there or when they were worshipping together, but outside of that he didn't really feel the need to.

His father also told him that Ross would be there on his journey too. He wouldn't be travelling the entire distance with him or any distance at all, but he would appear.[92] It seemed like he appeared at random times, but it was always at just the right moment. When he came he would offer a hand or give some encouragement or give a word from the LORD, just as he had always done while Timothy was growing up and even before that. At least, that was according to his great grandfather. Ross had been there for them too. He came often, not just to check on their physical status, but to check on their spiritual status. The resurrected saints were like that. They were constantly overseeing, judging and caring for those alive during this era, the Millennium. Timothy didn't know too many of the saints, because he had never left The Aarde Daal, but when he was a boy Ross had told him about many others who were also helping to rule the people in God's great kingdom.[93]

Timothy remembered Ross telling him of a woman named Louise, she too had been faithful to God during her life on earth. Ross and Louise had been married,[94] but of course, after they had died and then were resurrected, they were no longer considered to be married, for they were married to the Lamb of God.[95] They were kind of like angels, but they weren't angels. Their bodies looked like human bodies and yet they were different, they were glorified bodies.[96] Father had tried to explain how they were transformed, conformed, into God's image,[97] to look as He did, and to exemplify His character and to shine with His glory. Their bodies were immortal, imperishable,[98] they did not wear down as the human bodies did. Mind you it took hundreds of years for the human body to show signs of aging, but those who were resurrected, never aged. And they were spiritual, oh so spiritual,[99] even more spiritual than his father, grandfather, and great grandfather, who were always speaking of and praising the name of the LORD. The resurrected saints were nice to have around. It was nice to have their guidance on a regular basis. He would miss Ross' wisdom and care given during his regular visits. He was thankful that he would "drop" in every once in a while, yet he was also a bit apprehensive. What if he found out the truth? Without his family there to help with the spiritual talk what if he couldn't convince Ross he was genuine? What if he turned out not to be worthy? Would Ross stop him from going to Jerusalem? Would he send him home? Timothy dared not hope, that would be an utter disgrace and yet a relief all at the same time.

Louise, the other resurrected saint that Ross spoke of, did not live in the Aarde Daal, or even on their continent. Her role in reigning with Christ kept her closer to Zion. She too had been faithful and God had given her an area to work. Of course Ross would see her when he returned to the New Jerusalem, which was located over the old Jerusalem.[100] That was where their "home" was, or more like their base. They would worship the LORD, fellowship with other resurrected saints, learn new things about God, learn of new tasks to be done, rest up, and serve in any way possible. They would then leave from there to complete their assignment or check on those people in their territories.

Timothy waved to his neighbors as he passed their house. The Todds had a wooden house that they had built toward the front of their property. Their farm looked like a village of its own, because each family had a little wooden cottage with their own garden beside each house. The houses were similar to Timothy's family; however, the Steade's homes were grouped closer together, in a cluster on one part of the property, unlike the Todds' homes. His father and grandfathers believed that they should be united, as one, and that living closer together, working together and talking about God together would keep them closer as a family and serving the LORD more. Timothy had never minded. He always loved the busyness of work and family life going on around him. There was such joy when everyone was gathered together and greater joy when you knew each other's needs and could easily help one another out. His love was the field, so Timothy was only too glad to work on some extra land, not just his garden or his parents' garden.

Timothy glanced about the Todds' land. The new house stood close to the road on the far east side of the property. It was the last house in their territory before the great forest. Their property seemed to phase naturally from garden to forest. There was no fence or dividing line between the two. Their animals were free to eat of the vegetation in the forest or to roam on their own land and graze on the succulent grass. The forest animals were also free to do the same. Timothy wondered if they often found many forest animals in their gardens.

The Todds' had just had another child, an additional boy. Such joy he brought to their home. Their oldest son was now two and he was a roamer. He loved the outdoors. Mark was his name. Timothy could see him hunkered by a hole in the grass. It appeared to be a viper's den. Sure enough, there just behind Mark slithered the beautiful snake. You could almost make out each triangular scale as it effortlessly weaved its way through the grass onto the sandy area beside Mark. Mark's face lit up with joy as he saw the viper approach him.[101] He loved the reds, oranges and yellows on the snake's body. It was almost as if someone had taken a brush and tried to blend the colors together where they met along the snake's back.

Mark petted the snake and watched it as it slithered into its hole. Timothy chuckled to himself. He guessed if he had been Mark he would have enjoyed playing with the viper too. Mark probably wished he could become a snake and fit down into the hole, just to spend time with it.

Ah, the joys of childhood and the time you could take to really enjoy all aspects of life.

As he walked, Timothy remembered a story that David, Mark's father, had told him. David's wife, Esther had been hanging laundry out to dry. Mark couldn't have been more than 3-4 months old at that time. He was just old enough to really start watching and noticing things and wanting to hold them or touch them himself. Esther had put Mark near some rocks where some cobras were sunning. Mark's eyes remained glued to the cobras. His little arms and legs would start jumping and moving in excitement and he made gurgling sounds as he tried his best to get to those beautiful creatures. David had told just how fascinated Mark had been. That Sabbath when they met, David gave praise to God that his child would grow up to appreciate the beauty of God's creation, especially the animals. He was impressed that his son would start at such a young age. Everyone in town who had heard the story praised God for this young boy's soft heart towards God's creation.

Timothy supposed that since Mark was growing up close to the forest, he probably got to see more animals than other families or children. It wasn't that the animals couldn't come out of the forest and onto their property, but they so preferred it in there that they just didn't wander out very often. They loved the place that God had created for them, it provided for all of their needs, their homes, food, and play. Perhaps Mark would gain a far greater appreciation for animals than Timothy had, because of his close proximity to the forest, or perhaps David was right and he was just born with a sensitive heart that would cherish God's creation.

Timothy adjusted the lamb in his arms again. The little thing just lay there, completely content and secure with Timothy carrying him. Not even the pausing to watch Mark with the viper had disturbed this little fellow. Maybe it would not be so difficult to care for this lamb on the journey; although, the journey was just beginning and he had a long way to go.

Timothy gave one last wave to Mark as he entered into the bright green forest. It would be about a two day trek through the thickest part of the forest before he came to another town. There was a narrow trail cut through the woods; it was about the width of two people across. Of course, with so many travelers each year to Zion, the trail was well used and the ground well trodden. It wasn't as if only his jurisdiction used the trail, there were many other families much farther south and west that would eventually trek through this land. They would pass by his home and the village and enter into the forest. Many of those travelling would stop at his family's home and spend the night, or gain some nourishment before continuing on their journey. It was something that always occurred this time of year. Timothy was used to these visitors. However, now instead of accepting visitors, it would be his turn to be the visitor, the one travelling on the journey to Zion.

The forest was darker and cooler than the bright open sunlight since the lush, tall trees blocked out much of the sun. The sun did manage to beam through little gaps between the leaves, like bouncing reflections of crystal from a prism. The bushy vegetation all around him was vibrant with color. There were various shades of green with colored flowers or ripe fruit growing on the plants. Numerous colored lizards and insects could be spotted on many branches and leaves, as well as buzzing through the air. The earth was black and damp from the night's dew. And there were many sounds from animals in the distance, making cheerful greetings to each other after a restful night's sleep. In the distance he could see birds flittering back and forth, sharing the joyous news that a delicious breakfast had been located. Just then Timothy looked up at a tree near him and spotted a little monkey. He was not much bigger than his little lamb. He was black with white around both of his eyes and had a whitish pink mouth. His soft black hair was spiked across the top of his head. His hair was thin and fluffy looking, just like a young baby's. His belly was grayish pink and the fur made an hour glass shape on his chest and stomach. He was calmly sitting on his branch observing Timothy and the little lamb. It was almost as if he was checking up on him as he walked. Timothy paused to get a better look at it. He really was a fascinating looking monkey. The little monkey seemed to give him a final smile then hopped off the branch and onto the next tree. He jumped from tree to tree making joyful sounds as he went. He seemed to be headed in the same direction as Timothy.

The monkey's movement propelled Timothy's feet forward. He followed the monkey while enjoying the sights and sounds of the forest. He continued walking for quite some time, not resting until he spotted a quick flowing stream to the left. It bubbled over the rocks sounding like laughter as it went. There were a few patches of grass near the stream and some ripe berries so Timothy decided to stop for lunch. He could hear his father's voice now, telling him to be sure and give the lamb plenty to eat and time to exercise. The sun was still shining brightly through the trees, making little patterns on the path and on the underbrush. Timothy carefully rested the little lamb on a patch of grass. The lamb sniffed around some before he decided to nibble on it.

Timothy took off his pack and reached for some of the bread his mother had sent. He picked some fresh berries growing nearby and ate them with his lunch. He removed a cup from the side of his bag and scooped some water from the stream. Drinking from the cool water, he now felt refreshed. He offered some water to the little lamb and was mesmerized while he watched him try to drink from the cup. It was quite a sight. The lamb seemed so perfectly content. He grazed on the grass before him, drank what was given to him, and was easily carried without making a fuss. It seemed that he might even be easier to care for than Timothy first thought, maybe even easier than caring for his beloved garden. Imagine that!

Timothy watched the lamb a little while longer. He really was perfect, steady little legs to walk on, short little ears that perked at Timothy's movements or when something in the distance caught his interest, and little black eyes set in his white face that were completely filled with trust. This little lamb really was something.

"You know, you just look as content as can be. You don't even seem to care that you are no longer around your mother or with your friends. How do you do it?"

After a few more minutes Timothy carefully picked up the lamb, folding his legs so he would not hurt them during the rest of the day's journey. The question he had asked the lamb was left unanswered as it continued to swirl through Timothy's mind.

Once again they were off, Timothy walking steadily, the little lamb lying contentedly in his arms, head poked out enjoying the scene as they trekked on. It really was a beautiful scene. There was constant movement in the forest, snakes slithering in the dust, mice scurrying about, pausing only to take a nibble here and there. There were birds swooping and gliding through the trees, occasionally landing on branches to sing a joyful tune. Little lizards, geckos, and hundreds of colorful insects of all shapes and sizes ran up and down the trees, busily working and eating. He even thought he saw some deer and zebra in the distance working away at their lunch. The forest was a beautiful and happy sight.

The day passed by as he steadily walked along carrying the little lamb. It didn't seem like too long before he knew it would be time to make camp and rest for the night. The forest was graying as only drops of orange glow peeked its way through the trees. Timothy found a patch of brush with some soft dirt. It was nestled in the upper roots of a large tree. He set the lamb beside the tree to graze on the bush and grass nearby. While the little lamb nibbled Timothy smoothed out the ground, removing a few rocks and twigs and spread out the blanket his mother had made for him. He used his jacket as a pillow, folding it over a couple of times to increase its height. When his makeshift bed was ready he took out some food and ate his evening meal. He did not see nor hear a stream nearby so he drank from the precious reserves he carried with him in his canteen. After he drank he shared some with the lamb.

Once the lamb had sufficient time to stretch his legs, Timothy gathered him close to his chest on the solid blanket and laid down on his right side to sleep. He had no fear in the woods; he knew it was safe,[102] for all of the animals were friendly.

The emotional strain and his walk that day had taken its toll on Timothy. All of the walking and observing of new things had kept his mind very busy. The warmth of the lamb next to him added to his comfort and soon all of the travel, the concern about the journey and what he would be required to do at the end of the journey faded from his mind. That "fear" of his unworthiness would have to be dealt with as he approached Zion, for now, he would just travel. Within a matter of minutes he was fast

Quest for a True Heart

asleep. He slept peacefully, a peace that could only come from the Spirit of God,[103] as if he were back in his own bed at home, next to his family and his beloved garden.

In the wee hours of the morning Timothy slowly stirred and stretched. He could feel the warmth from the lamb still snuggled against his chest, but there was another warm feeling against his back. He had a strange feeling that they were not alone, there seemed to be a large presence of something behind him. Although the nights were slowly cooling down, he had not felt the need for an extra blanket to cover himself or the lamb, so he hadn't used one, yet he was sure he felt something there.

As he sat up on his right elbow, careful not to disturb or hurt the lamb in any way, he caught a glimpse of what it was that was radiating heat and blocking him in. There, during the night, a reddish brown wolf[104] had found them snuggled at the base of the tree and decided to join them for a nap. The colors made diamond like shaped patterns on the front of him. His chest, neck and paws consisted of thin, soft, white fur. His tall triangular ears, forever perked up and rotating, were always listening, even in sleep, in case some great news came through the forest. He wasn't too large, a little older than a pup, maybe two or three years old. He was an intelligent looking animal. Perhaps this could be another companion on their journey, as the monkey had been yesterday, at least until they reached the edge of the forest tonight.

"Hey, there pup." Timothy said as he gently stroked the pup's neck. "Are you enjoying our bed? I don't suppose it's too often that you get to sleep on a blanket." Timothy rose as he chuckled. He then bent down to wake the lamb and see that he was fed, watered, and exercised.

The wolf stretched his long legs and yawned. His jaw opened wide enough to display all of his teeth and his long tongue. Timothy had heard about their long tongues, but he had never really taken the time to notice because he was always preoccupied with the plants in his garden and removing animal footprints.

Timothy ate some of the food his mother had sent for him, along with some fruit he had discovered on the path yesterday. He was most excited about the varieties and decided he would get some cuttings on his way back for his garden. He drank from his canister and again gave some to the lamb. The wolf, which had now fully awakened was walking around and also came to Timothy for a drink.

"Well, alright, you can have some, on the condition that you point out the next nearest stream so I can refill my canister." The wolf had a gleam in his eyes and lowered his head just a bit; perhaps that was as close to a yes as Timothy would get. He poured out some of his water into the wolf's mouth.

The trio journeyed on for the better part of the day. They ate together, walked together, and sometimes, talked together, well, sort of. Timothy felt a little strange talking to animals. He was used to being alone and thinking aloud to himself about his plants.

Later that day, the wolf kept his end of the bargain and showed Timothy and the lamb to a beautiful stream with a mini waterfall. They were all able to enjoy a wonderful lunch filled with various fruits and to relax while watching numerous animals along the stream as they flitted or walked about looking for food. Timothy started to take more notice of the animals, not because they interested him any more than they had before, but because they revealed an assortment of plants that seemed to be hidden from his eyesight.

As the day came to a close Timothy noticed the forest seemed to be thinning and the light from above lit more of the path. When the wolf saw the opening up ahead he gave a little yelp, as if to say goodbye, then turned and ran back through the thick forest.

Chapter 7

Timothy walked into the clearing at dusk. A few tree branches lumbered over him as he gazed at the little town before him. It was similarly set up like Aarde Daal. The homes were divided on different properties. Each spacious piece of land had homes built by the families and gardens large enough to supply the family and travelers with food.[105] Animals were scattered here and there, lambs and cows grazed on the grass, monkeys swung from trees, lizards ran up and down the paths, snakes slithered through the grass and parrots squawked from roof and tree tops. They all appeared to be calming down and settling in for the night.

Timothy noticed a few people moving about. They were finishing up their final chores for the day and going to be heading home soon. One particular man carrying a straw basket of fruit caught Timothy's attention. The trees on the left in the first yard were laden with brightly colored fruit. The branches hung low bearing the weight of the ripened fruit that awaited picking. Timothy couldn't help but notice the fine quality of the fruit. He strode over to the man with purpose in his steps, "Sir, do you need any help carrying these in?" Timothy asked, referring to a number of baskets on the back of a large cart.

"Thanks, that would be great," the tall, thin man replied.

Timothy set down his sack and the little lamb, allowing him to roam around. He wanted the lamb to have a chance to eat as well as stretch his scrawny legs. But most importantly he wanted an up close look at this beautiful fruit. It was a waxy yellow in color and feel and it was oddly shaped. It had a center with five points protruding from it. Timothy grabbed a basket and followed the man into the storage barn. "You look like you have an excellent crop this year. Your trees are so full and bright with fruit. I have never seen these before, what are they called?"

"Yes, we have been blessed. God has seen fit to multiply our crops, just as He has promised.[106] He is so faithful.[107] I've seen His care for more than 200 years. He will not let His people down." He looked up and offered a silent praise before he continued. "This fruit is carambola. I received it from some travelers from the south many years ago. They used to pass this way when they would go to Jerusalem. We would always have such wonderful times together praising God. On one of their trips they brought me some seeds and a sample plant as a thank you for all the time that they had spent here."

"It looks interesting, such a bright yellow. Is the coating actually wax?"

"No, not wax, just the skin. We actually call them star fruit because of their shape, they are wonderfully tasty. Please, try one. It reminds me of a pineapple however, it does not have a strong flavor. It's very mellow and very juicy when ripe."

"Thank you."

"I would guess that you are travelling to Jerusalem. Am I correct?" the man asked, as he carefully set his basket near the shed wall. He motioned for Timothy to put his basket next to his then they headed back out to the wooden cart to retrieve another one.

"Yes, I began my journey two days ago. I have only passed through the forest between your territory and mine. This is my first journey."

"Ah, 'tis a journey you will never forget. I am fortunate to have accompanied my father on his journey a couple of times. As I am not the eldest, I have not had the express privilege of taking the journey myself and standing in as the head of my home. You are so fortunate to be the leader of your home. What a blessing from God. You truly can magnify the Lord and exalt Him with praise."

"Uh, yeah," Timothy hesitated as he tried not to sound too negative, "It sure is a blessing."

The man continued on, as if barely hearing Timothy's response. "I remember the first time I saw the city of Zion. The glow from the throne could be seen far beyond the city limits. It was as if the sun itself was sitting in Jerusalem."

"Wow, that bright? I had always heard His glory shone throughout the city."

"Oh yes, what magnificent, pure glory, pure brightness. You can't even imagine it unless you've seen it. It's just absolutely incredible. The land is vibrant, the people excitable. The energy in the air surpasses anything you will ever feel anywhere else. And the people and Resurrected Saints… why the atmosphere just proclaims who Christ is. It is positively the most wonderful place to be." His face was turned toward the sky; he was lost in his memories.

"That will be interesting to see. My great-grandfather speaks of it all of the time. He simply proclaims over and over again the magnificence of the city and of the LORD. That is all he dwells on. I always supposed it was because he represented the family the longest and he was one of the first to see such drastic changes from what the world was, before, you know."

"I suppose that has something to do with it, but I think you'll understand more once you see if for yourself. I know that I could not begin to imagine what it was like until I went myself. As wonderful as this earth is, it is pale in comparison to what you will see and experience."

They were finishing up with the last of the baskets when the man finally turned to shake Timothy's hand and give him a brotherly embrace. "I'm sorry, I didn't even introduce myself. So caught up was I in our conversation. I'm Bahaudeen,[108] faithful servant of the Most High God.

Thank you for your help. Please know that you are more than welcome to stay with my family and I for the night, we would consider it an honor to house a representative in our home. You can tell me all about yourself and your excitement about seeing the city over dinner."

"Why thank you. I appreciate it. I'm Timothy. Uh, what should I do with this lamb?"

"Your sacrifice, yes. Well, you must bring him in, we must take great care of God's sacrifice, it is to have no spot or blemish. So we must protect and care for it. Let's grab some straw, grain, and fresh grass for him. He looks fairly young, so he'll do best with the grains. We'll put it in your room for the night. There he will have a comfortable place to stay while we visit."

Inside? The house? Timothy wanted to protest, but the man's facial expression and actions showed he was truly serious. Bahaudeen had already begun to move the straw and carry it through the house. Timothy hadn't ever heard of bringing animals into a house before. But then again, most people who journeyed past his house came from farther away than Timothy, so carrying an animal that distance just wasn't practical. Although he had to admit that he didn't really pay attention to the people or animals that stayed over. He never really thought about it before. He figured if they didn't have an animal than they would just purchase one when they got to Jerusalem. He didn't see how it made much difference, but either way, keeping animals in the house was definitely not something he was accustomed to, nor was it an idea he thought he would like when he retired for the night. It wasn't like the sheep was likely to come to any harm outside or in the barn. All the animals got along just fine (tame and wild).

Timothy shook his head as he followed Bahaudeen through the wooden house into a room in the back. It was overlooking the forest, not his favorite view, but it would do. He would much rather look over the man's fields or his orchards. Then he could study his land and see how it was laid out. Perhaps he could get some creative ideas to use when he returned home. They placed the hay and fresh grass they had gathered in the corner and set up some bowls with grain and water. Timothy then removed his few belongings and laid them on the edge of the bed. He noticed that the lamb had followed them in without even being called or carried. He seemed to follow Timothy wherever he went. Interesting behavior after just two days, considering he had nothing to do with the lamb before. Perhaps the lamb was just missing its mother.

Timothy chuckled a bit to himself. "Would you look at that, he followed us right in here."

"You must be a good shepherd, for this little lamb knows his master well and follows him wherever he goes. Sheep always follow their trustworthy shepherd."

He paused for a moment as Timothy looked at the lamb. "Shepherd, me," Timothy thought to himself, "Not me, I'm a farmer, gardener, worker of the fields. Don't get yourself confused little lamb, I am no shepherd."

"Hey, let me introduce you to my wife then I'll show you where to wash up for dinner."

Chapter 8

Timothy was soon settled in and enjoying the simple dinner. Their conversation was anything but simple as Bahaudeen shared stories of his trips to Jerusalem. It made Timothy feel a little uncomfortable.

"I remember one year in particular, I think it was my third trip with my father and grandfather, we always travelled together as a family. I think that is what made it even more special, the time we spent together and the memories we made.

I remember that I had always been in awe of everything around me, the sights, the sounds, but most impressive was the feeling in the air, the atmosphere. There were feelings of peace and joy that flowed over me. I had let myself lose focus that year, taking up my time with other things, but I remember as I neared the city, all of those feelings disappeared. It became obvious that my little life was not meant to be taken up with other concerns or tasks, but to be spent in worship. It became so clear and real to me that week. We were camped on the side of a hill, south of Jerusalem.

There were hundreds of thousands of people all gathered to worship and they would sing in the camps around the city. It made every other song you've ever heard sound muted and quiet compared to the thousands upon thousands of singing voices. They would join as one and lift their voices upwards toward the city. You felt like you could have floated on the notes. All my cares floated away that week and I realized just how amazing it felt to serve Him."

"My sister would love that, she loves it when our town gathers and sings praises. I think she was born for singing."

"That's a good possibility, God gives each person gifts to use in worship to Him and He surely loves to see us use them and to hear praises sung to His name. Another memory that I have from that year was that we happened to camp near a group of men who had uncovered an old book. It had the words, "Holy Bible" written across the black leather cover. They had been sharing it and reading portions of what is called the Old Testament. It's a series of books about the history of God's people. Well, the stories they would tell about God's power from that book… I wish I had lived in days of old. The stories were incredible. Imagine - to see God use an old shepherd, sent away because he killed someone, and he was to help free the entire Israeli nation. What a terrible act, but God still chose to use him. Of course, the leader from Egypt was furious and wouldn't let him take the people. I can't imagine what that would have looked like, I mean, think about it. Really, someone willing to definitely disobey God and His plan? Unheard of! They kept saying that his heart was hardened, but in the end God dealt with him."

"That is a strange thought. I can't imagine anyone even thinking of being so outright disobedient, let alone acting that rudely. I know my great grandfather has shared some stories of the way things were before Christ came to reign, but I cannot imagine what that would really look like. People just don't act that way."

"Anyway, the leader was so stubborn, according to the men, that God decided to send plagues to change his mind."

"Plagues? What are those?"

"Like punishments for not listening, terrible things happened. But the thing is God didn't just send the punishment to the leader, he sent it to everyone, his entire nation and some of the punishments overflowed onto God's own people!"

"What kind of punishment or plague did He send?"

"He actually sent ten of these plagues."

"Ten!?! On His own people too?"

"Yes, ten. The first one was turning all of the water into blood. I remember as I walked back with my dad through Egypt how amazed I was. We decided to walk the trail since hearing these stories, rather than take the boat. Think about it. The Nile River flows all the way down, Egypt, over 4000 miles. You'll see it if you take the land route up to Jerusalem. Just think, every little bit of water for farming, drinking, cooking and everything was turned to blood, over the entire land. The power that God used to do that, just to show this leader that He wanted His people, is so great!"

"But water is so necessary for survival. How could anyone survive? What about the crops? They would need to transport that water to sustain their farms." The farmer in him came out with all the drastic effects no water would have on plants. He had thought of the possibility before, his grandfather always reminded him about the size of the pond and the blessing that came with sending a representative to Jerusalem, however, he could never fully believe that such a thing, as not having water, would ever actually happen.

"I know. The animals too and the fish in the water, could you imagine all of the damage caused by such a change?"

"No, how could God allow all of that destruction to His creation. Why, when it could be so beautiful? It didn't do anything. I hope that leader changed his mind."

"Well, that's the thing. He said he was going to, but then when the blood was changed back he wouldn't let the Israelites go. So God used this man Moses and He sent another plague. There were frogs everywhere. Imagine, God, calling all of the frogs to go and descend upon Egypt?"

"Frogs, why frogs? They would eat all the insects that are used for pollinating plants. Long term, your crops would die. Wouldn't that hurt everyone?"

Bauhadeen was so into his story now that he didn't notice Timothy's question. "But that wasn't the worst. Each time their leader would still go against God, he would not let God's people go. They had lice, flies, their cattle died from pestilence; they had boils all over themselves, hailstones (ice) that fell from the sky, locust that ate whatever survived from the other plagues, and great darkness, so dark that you could not even see with a light, it just wouldn't shine through."

"I don't know what to be more impressed with. The list of things that God did or the stubbornness of this leader that he would endure all this punishment and not let God's people go. I'm sure his own people must have had something to say to him. Didn't he know he couldn't win? I mean, his land was already in ruins, what else did he have to lose? I can't imagine a land so ruined. It would be worthless. His kingdom would not be able to sustain itself."

"The final plague was the one that has the most significant effect. If I understood the men correctly, they seemed to think that God wanted this leader to go through all of this so that this last plague would happen and be an example for thousands of years to come, even for us today in this era. It would have the greatest effect."

"What do you mean? How could one plague, like frogs or flies or darkness have an effect for years to come, other than it let some people get frustrated and others leave and establish themselves in a new country? What was the last plague?"

"The last plague was that the firstborn in EVERY family was to die, in the livestock, and in the Israelite camp.[109] God had a different plan. He told the Israelites that if they wanted to save their firstborn something would have to die in the eldest's place. And so, a lamb was killed. A poor innocent lamb that had no part in this leader's thinking or in any Israelite's thinking. The lamb had done nothing at all, but to God, it was a very important part of His plan. This lamb would be the sacrifice, to die for the firstborn. Its blood would be spread on the doorposts outside to show that death had come to that house."

"That doesn't seem right."

"No, but a sacrifice was needed nonetheless. So the lamb was killed, its blood was spread on the doorposts and its meat eaten that night and the firstborn lived."

"So you're saying that God was showing that He was providing the sacrificial lamb? And from this He would show that one day He would die in the people's place, like the lamb died for the Israelite family?"

"Yes."

"Well, everyone knows that God sacrificed His Son for man, even if they don't know the story about this leader from Egypt and the lamb that had to be killed. So are you just amazed at all that God was able to do with the plagues?"

"Yes and no. I was amazed at God's power, I always am. To think that He can act and control all of these little things for this king and to know how He controls this world to keep it from evil now amazes me. He orchestrates our lives. He is so interested in everything, little or large that goes on with His people. Once you see Him in Jerusalem you too will be amazed. He is a great God. How could One so mighty and powerful willingly give up His Son to die as the sacrificial lamb, like the little lamb you are carrying on your journey? I just can't understand how great He is for doing this for us. It just makes me want to praise Him ALL of the time!"

"Hmmm, I guess that is amazing. That this all powerful God gave His Son's life for us."

"More than amazing, it's incomprehensible."

There was a silence as Bahaudeen reflected on the greatness of God. It didn't matter how often he thought of it or talked about it with others, God's great love for him always amazed him. He was so undeserving, yet he felt so loved and worthy because of the King. Timothy was beginning to feel uncomfortable as the silence stretched on. Thankfully Bahaudeen's wife spoke up.

Quest for a True Heart

"Yes dear, you are right," Bahaudeen's wife stated as she stood to clear the dishes, "God dying for anyone is not a thing anyone can grasp. So let us be grateful and live well for Him with much gratitude. Now, why don't you two go outside and enjoy some of His beautiful gifts to you before the evening gets too much later? The stars are so beautiful."

With a chuckle and a kiss for his wife Bahaudeen took Timothy out to show him the stars and some of his garden areas near the house. Timothy was quite impressed with the health and abundance of his produce and he took careful mental notes about some of the things he wanted to include on his own property when he returned home.

"Have you ever heard of the garden that God made for the first people He created?" Bahaudeen asked.

"Oh yes, the Garden of Eden. It was perfect. I often try to imagine what that looked like. I think it would be the perfect way to set up our property at home, trees all around, with certain ones in the middle and a spring of water bubbling up forming a river that branches off onto other properties. Everything would be lush and green and the fruit always ripe for the harvest. Yes indeed, I know of this garden well. Gardening is my passion."

"Yes, it would be an excellent set-up for your property, however, that is not what this garden is best known for."

"Oh no, of course not."

"You see that garden was where God first mentioned sacrifice. It is where the first death took place. It's the theme that runs through the "Holy Bible", it tells the purpose of life."

"Really?" questioned Timothy. He wondered if Bahaudeen was obsessed with sacrifices. That seemed to be where most of his conversations ended up. He wondered why. There were no animal killings now. All creatures worked together in harmony, just like the people. So, why this talk of death all of the time?

"Well, the first people disobeyed in the garden, so that separated them from God. Thankfully we live in a society and world today where there is not that same kind of evil or separation. I'm thankful God has it all under control. I would not want to live in a world apart from Him."

"From the few stories my great grandfather told me about the battles he fought and the evil running rampant on the earth, yes, I would have to agree that God now has everything under control. It had to have taken great power to clean this place up."

"Yes, and death."

"So how does death, which is evil, get rid of evil?"

"It's the punishment, the consequence. When something wrong happens, something must step in to fix it. Death was the punishment for evil, so something had to take the place of death in order for the other person to survive. At first it was the death of an animal, but really, that was only temporary, there had to be something greater that would last. So, the Son came."

"This is why He died, for everyone?"

"Yes, to take away the separation."

"Okay."

"No, not okay!" Bahaudeen was getting emotional, "It's not okay. Don't you see?"

Timothy looked at him blankly. "See what?" He wondered. Why such a big deal. He knew God had sent His Son to die for everyone. Everyone knew about God.[110]

"God is not just a lamb or a calf or some animal, God is this all-powerful, amazing being. To see Him sitting on His throne in Jerusalem is to see the greatest thing in the universe and beyond. You have seen nothing greater."

"O-k-ay." Timothy replied hesitantly, he wasn't sure what to say. He knew this information, at least most of it was buried deep somewhere in his head. What he didn't get was why Bahaudeen was getting so excited about it all. What difference did it make?

"You'll see." Bahaudeen stated, as if he had a point to make that his pupil just wasn't understanding, "Once you get to Jerusalem, you'll understand. There is nothing better, there is nothing greater, He is IT!"

They walked back to the house in silence. Not really seeing eye to eye. Not understanding each other's perspective. Timothy didn't say much. He felt worse than ever. If he couldn't understand why this simple concept was so important how was he ever going to make it in Jerusalem? Why did death in a perfect world matter? If everything was running so well, why ruin it with doom, gloom and despair? Why say that death was still the punishment? Wasn't that taken care of? Didn't the King who reigned have everything under control?

With so many questions swirling in his mind Timothy was beginning to feel dizzy. When they reached the house he pleaded tiredness and headed to his room. The little lamb was lying comfortably on his straw. He looked up at Timothy as he walked in, his large eyes waiting in response of his master. How could Timothy do this? This little lamb was so innocent, so pure. Death didn't make sense. Was this all some tradition, something he was forced to do because it had been done for thousands of years? Was that the purpose of Bahaudeen sharing these stories? Or was there something more? Timothy didn't know. At 85 years old, he just wasn't sure. What if, when he got there, these questions went against him? His lack of faith would surely be pinpointed. What then? What was he to say to his family? Would there really be problems if he didn't go through with the sacrifice? He sure felt like he was inadequate and not going to represent his family well. Maybe he should turn back in the morning and tell his father he needed to go instead. Maybe he should leave now.

Chapter 9

As Timothy readied for bed he reflected on what had been said at the table and on the walk. His view of God seemed so insignificant in comparison to his family's and definitely to Bahaudeen's view. He simply could not comprehend how a God so great could stoop so low and be such a sacrifice as a little lamb. Nor why it would matter so much. If it really mattered, why didn't God just take care of it so there need not be any sacrifice or travelling? He could do it, couldn't He? Perhaps if it didn't fall at this time of year, maybe if it was during the time well before harvest and planting, but not around tilling season…

He whipped back the sheets on the bed in frustration and crawled under. The little lamb didn't hesitate, he waited just a moment for Timothy to get comfortable and still, then jumped up on the bed and nestled down right next to Timothy, as he had for the past two nights.

"Yeesh! It sure didn't take too long for you to find out what's comfortable." Timothy groaned and then rolled over and closed his eyes in frustration. This just wasn't coming easily. It wasn't like he could just make these feelings appear. It wasn't like he could understand. Why should it matter?

Timothy was at least grateful for a bed that night although he slept fitfully with his little lamb constantly at his side. He rose early the next morning and straightened the room. He decided the best thing to do was to get out of here quickly. Forget the information about the plants, gardens, and fruit. He just needed to get back on the path and get this job over with.

"Good morning," he greeted Bahaudeen, "How was your night?"

"In peace I will lie down and sleep, for You alone, O Lord make me to dwell in safety.[111]"

"That's nice that you slept well." Timothy commented. He tried not to sound too disgusted or discouraged.

"Are you ready for a delicious breakfast? My dear wife sure can cook and always out does herself when we have company. I guess secretly that might be another reason I like this time of year, the food is better," he gave a small chuckle and smiled as they rounded the corner into the kitchen area.

"Good morning, 'how blessed is the man whose strength is in You, in whose heart are the highways *to Zion*!'[112]"

"Thank you, my dear, what a beautiful blessing."

"Come, sit and enjoy. Please eat as much as you like and I'll wrap the leftovers up for you to take with you."

"Thank you, I appreciate that."

"Past here is about a three day walk before the next settlement."

Timothy quickly ate his fill, grateful for the delicious tasting food, but anxious to get going before another conversation could develop. He said his farewells and gave the home a blessing as was customary, "'May you be blessed of the Lord, Maker of heaven and earth'.[113]" With that, he headed out once again, bag filled with leftovers and the little lamb in his arms.

The forest looked the same as the west side had, very vibrant, colorful and full of life. He walked quickly, trying to make the best time possible and escape the questions that kept nagging him. He knew he had to complete this journey. He knew it was important to his family. He mostly knew what to expect when he got there, what he had to do. But the purpose, the reason it was so important, that he could not get his mind around. He had always been told this is what brought the blessing of rain, so for rain, he would do it. But, he just wasn't sure or at least as sure as his family that it was what really made the difference.

It wasn't until the end of his second day of travelling through the forest that he began to notice some subtle changes. There seemed to be fewer plants and animals than he had seen the day before. There also seemed to be more sunlight from above, which he thought was nice, since he could walk for a bit longer in the evenings because the trees allowed more light to peek through. Things looked a little sparse. "Perhaps," he thought, "I have travelled quicker than I thought and will reach the next territory tonight."

The little lamb started to squirm a bit. Timothy figured it was probably getting tired from being carried. The poor little thing wasn't used to doing very little, it was used to walking and jumping around its mother all day, but Timothy didn't want anything to happen to it, he knew it could not be hurt in any way for it to be offered for a sacrifice. He didn't want to bring it all that distance just to be told to take it home again. He figured it would be okay for the lamb to walk for a little bit, so long as he kept a close eye on it.

He set the lamb down on the dirt path. The lamb looked around for a second and then began following him. Timothy had slowed his pace down in order to keep a close eye on it. He shouldn't have worried. The lamb was careful and followed closely. There wasn't any grass around, so the lamb didn't stop to munch or sniff. They walked for another hour before Timothy decided to stop for the night. He found a tiny strip of grass where the lamb could feed and he ended up eating the last of the food that Bahaudeen had given him. He hadn't found any berries that whole day and where they were stopped he couldn't see any either. Because he didn't hear any ripples or sounds from a stream he decided not to look around. He knew he should be in the next territory by mid-day tomorrow or even early morning since he had walked so quickly and steadily, so he was sure he could fill up his canteen and find some food there.

The patch of ground that he decided to lay on was harder than the night before. There were extra stones in the dirt and he just couldn't make himself comfortable. Finally, well into the night he fell asleep. He slept fitfully that night and so did his little lamb. He awoke slowly the next morning with a few kinks in his neck and back.

As he tried to stretch them out he mumbled to himself and the lamb, "Ugh, I feel rough. That wasn't exactly comfortable or restful. You know what? Let's just head into the next town. It can't be more than a few hours of walking. We're sure to be well fed and then we can spend the night there. I sure need a better night's rest than last night and so do you. I feel like I slept on every rock in the forest. That ground sure was hard. Besides, I think I'm ready for some socializing. This forest is too quiet for me. I need someone else to talk to other than a lamb." He picked up the lamb and began walking.

Around mid-morning the trees really began to thin out and he knew he had to be nearing the next territory. Within another half hour the clearing came into view. The trees at the edge of the forest were barren. *He remembered his great grandfather had described to him what deciduous trees looked like in the winter. He thought that these trees must look same. His great grandfather had been up north in what they used to call Eurasia, the land far above Jerusalem. It was before the Great War. He said the ground was bare, no grass, no leaves, no vibrant colors, just all brown, dismal, dark and dead. "It looked as life had disappeared forever. There were no animals scurrying to and fro. Even the air felt dead. There was a chill to the air, as if it threatened life itself- daring it to appear. The trees were masses of empty branches, no fruit, no leaves, and no birds. They were empty. All you could hear was the cold wind whipping through them, barring any life from returning."* A shiver ran down Timothy's back. He didn't think it could be winter here, even though he thought it looked similar to his great grandfather's description. As he approached the territory he noticed that there were a few leaves on the trees. They had brown fringes and their color was not full and vibrant green like he was used to.

The ground was hard and dry. All the trees were scantily clad with few leaves barely holding on. The ground seemed drier and lighter brown, like a sandy brown instead of the rich black earth he was accustomed to. He took in many of these changes as he approached the first acreage. Nature was a part of him, he loved it and lived for working the ground and seeing the bounty of his hard work. But, he could tell there was a stark difference between his home and the territory he now entered. Perhaps there was more of that 'winter' here that his great grandfather had described to him so long ago.

Timothy noticed that the houses were similar to the ones he was used to. Each house was built and lived in by immediate family members, gathered together on their families' property. Each home had a limited garden right beside it with few vegetables and he noticed there were a few animals lying around. But it lacked vibrancy and life, and that puzzled him. It just didn't look 'right', nor did it feel right. It didn't look like the farms that he had been used to or like the one he had visited just a few days before. He had been so used to farms where the lushness and bounty were prevalent. But here, here was different. He supposed it was only because he was a gardener that he noticed such a stark contrast. Perhaps it wasn't that different. Maybe, once he was on someone's property and could walk around, it wouldn't be as drastic as he first thought. Or maybe no one lived here or cared for the place.

It was then that he noticed a man walking towards him from the rustic, wooden home. He was tall and thin. His hair was graying and his straw hat had frayed. There was gray stubble on his chin and the tan, creased lines from his eyes seemed to wrinkle his entire face. He seemed like a friendly man, yet there seemed to be something missing, some energy or vibrancy or something. What it was Timothy could not figure out, but he knew there was something different.

"Good day to you traveler, how are you this fine day?" the man questioned.

"I am well sir. I am on my way to Jerusalem. Would it be possible for me to sojourn with you over the Sabbath?" Timothy let his hand rest gently on the lamb, stroking it unknowingly, while settling it down.

"Why of course. We do not have a great abundance, but what we have you are welcome to. Come, rest your belongings inside. What a nice lamb you have. I haven't seen one like that in many a year."

"He is a perfect little lamb. I am doing my best to care for him, although I am not a shepherd at heart. My love is the gardens. I would be happy to help you in yours until evening if you like."

"That would be wonderful, I would love the help. Gardening is not my thing, as you may have noticed. Personally, I prefer other things, but, you have to grow food to live, so the gardens must stay," he chuckled. "I'll be glad for whatever help I can get. My name's Amos."

"Timothy, pleasure to be here. Like I said, I'm headed to Jerusalem."

"I never did see reason why one should wear themselves out each year on such a long journey. Anyway, welcome. Come inside. Let's put your things down to rest, grab a bite to eat, and see what work we can get done while it's still daylight."

Timothy put the lamb down so he could find a place to graze. It had been a few hours since he had eaten. They hurriedly placed Timothy's belongings inside the house and grabbed a bite to eat.

Without any hesitation Timothy followed Amos to the fields and set to work. This was his passion, this was his love, this was where he wanted to be, in the fields working in nature. To him there was no greater place to be, no other place so peaceful and like home. He was glad that he had walked quickly and that he would have the better part of the day to spend it on doing what he liked best.

"This here territory is called Jacan.[114] It was given to me by my grandfather. Since my father left years ago he hasn't come out to work much. He just sits in his little house in the back corner. I check on him now and again and bring him food every few days. That's his little house over there." Amos pointed with his head as they walked to the largest garden plot. There stood a little black cottage with a rustic looking porch. In the background were a few trees that reached their bare branches above the forlorn house. There was a small pond in the front, fringed in light green grass. It was the brightest spot on the property, as far as Timothy could see at the moment. "This here is where I do my main growing. I don't plant too much, makes no sense as I don't care to garden and since it's only my grandfather, my wife and I. We don't need to eat that much."

Timothy took in the scene. There were rows and rows of hard packed soil. Where it was harvest time the field should have had leaves spilling out all over it and it should have been full of ripe vegetables, but it wasn't. There were only scrawny leaves and vines scattered here and there. The leaves were a faded green trimmed in brown and lifeless, drooping down to the ground as if they didn't have the energy to get up and soak in the sunlight.

"Where's your pond or well?" Timothy asked.

"Right over there, to the left. My grandfather has always loved the water, so he had to build his property near it so he could look at it every day. I think he especially likes to see the reflection of the sun setting in the evenings. He said the orange glow reminds him of something."

"Oh."

"I have some buckets here we can use to carry the water to the plants. I guess I should do it more often, but it's a lot of work."

"Perhaps we could rig up some sort of irrigation system. My great grandfather taught me how to hook up hoses and pipes to carry water to the garden. It sure cuts down on your work. He helped me set up one for a new area I was planting once. It was on a different part of our property, one that had not been used before, so I wanted to saturate it after I had planted my first crop there."

"Yeah? I think I have some hoses hanging around somewhere. If not, I could ask my grandfather. I'm sure he'd know. He used to love gardening and farming. It was he who did all this work before, but then he stopped and left it up to me."

"Okay. I see there is a slight decline, so that would help the water to naturally run down into the garden once the hoses are in place. We probably won't even need a pump."

They reached the top of the hill and looked out over the pond towards the forest from which Timothy had just come. The pond stretched a short distance across the top of the plateau. The grass around it was brighter green and healthier looking than the rest of the area. The pond appeared to be shallow, but Timothy figured it would work to transport the water to the garden and at least aid in the final growth process of those vegetables before they were harvested. Once they set up this simple system Timothy figured Amos could easily rig another irrigation system from his main watering pond for future use.

They rummaged through the little barn and found some hoses that would do the job. Timothy and Amos set to work fastening the hoses together and securing them to the ground so that animals would not come and move them from the water by accident. They found a manifold so they could attach three hoses and run them into three different areas of the garden. Within a few short hours they had the hoses connected and water running into the garden. Timothy had dug simple trenches to let the water spread further.

"Well, looks like we're nearing quitting time. You sure wore me out, just watching you makes me tired. We'll have to leave it as is until after the Sabbath. Let's head in and get cleaned up." He sounded anxious, like he couldn't wait to get away from the fields.

Reluctantly Timothy turned the water connection off, so the garden would not flood. Tomorrow being the Sabbath he knew he wouldn't be out here. No work could be done. It was important to rest. He knew they would be staying in and taking it easy. Oh how he longed to be out here. There was so much work to do. So much he knew he could help with. He had lots of advice and ways to fix up this property so it would start producing. He had so many ideas that he wanted to share with Amos. Although it had been less than a week, it felt like it had been ages since he had been working in his beloved garden. Thankfully he'd be here at least two days since he couldn't travel on the Sabbath. That was no hardship in Timothy's thinking. He would map out a plan of action that would get Amos' fields back on track. He wondered if it would be appropriate to discuss it with him on the Sabbath.

They cleaned up a bit outside by the well before heading in. As they were walking through the door Timothy heard a little noise. "Baa."

"Oh, my lamb. I was so intent on working the garden that I forgot all about this little guy."

"Oh yeah. Uh, you know where the barn is. You could find a stall, put some straw in there and lock him up for the night. He should be okay. I think we still have a little straw left in the top loft."

"Uh, thanks." Timothy picked up the lamb and stroked it. "The barn? Sorry little guy. It looks like we'll be separated for a little bit. You'll be okay. The barn is safe and I'll let you out in the morning." Timothy found an empty stall that was somewhat clean. In fact, all the stalls were empty. There were bits of hay strewn here and there and mud from someone's boots that had dried a long time ago. The barn looked deserted.

Timothy didn't have too much time before sunset to look around much more. He quickly set the lamb down and climbed the ladder to the loft. Amos was right. He had a little straw, very little. "This guy must really not like gardening of any sort. He's got next to nothing." Timothy thought to himself.

He was able to gather enough straw to make a bed for the lamb and give him some to nibble on, but it wasn't much. "I'll see you in the morning, okay?"

The lamb looked at Timothy with sorrow filled eyes. Timothy's conscience panged. "You'll be okay." With that he closed the gate and strode toward the house.

"Hi, you must be Timothy. I'm Wafiyyah,[115] but everyone calls me Fi. My husband said you are quite the worker. He says you have more zeal than 100 of him for the garden. Thanks for being willing to help him out. He really doesn't enjoy work outside of any kind." She smiled kindly as she moved toward the hallway. "Come, let me show you your room while you are here. You can finish cleaning up and supper will begin in about half an hour."

"Thank you." Timothy followed Fi down the hallway. He took in the simple surroundings. The wooden walls were bare, but clean. The room he entered had a single bed with a three drawer dresser and a bedside table. There was one light in the room. Faded green curtains hung over the windows. Timothy set his bag on the dresser, pulled out a clean change of clothes, and headed to wash up.

Quest for a True Heart

As he cleaned up, his mind worked on a plan. At his father's suggestion he had left home early for his trip. He knew he was only a week into it, however, he figured he could spare a couple of days and still make it to Jerusalem on time. What would it hurt if he stayed here for a few extra days? He could have Amos show him around the rest of his property. He could make sure the garden was well watered and doing better and then give him advice or a plan to work on while he was gone. Timothy knew that a little work every day was far better than a lot of work on one or two days. Plants needed constant care and a watchful hand. You couldn't just plant something and not return to it until it was harvest season, there had to be some looking in on the plants to see what was going on.

Timothy thought his idea sounded wonderful. Not only would he get a few extra days in the fields, but he would be helping a person in need. That had to count for something. He thought he'd mention his plan to Amos after dinner, not to discuss, just to think about it, seeing how it was the Sabbath, and let him know his thoughts later on.

They sat down to a simple meal. It was not nearly as elaborate as his breakfast had been at Bahaudeen's, but it was filling. As Fi cleaned up Timothy approached Amos about his idea.

"I was thinking. If you don't mind, I would like to stay for a few extra days after the Sabbath and help you out. I love working the land and I'm sure I could be some help to you before I continue on my journey. I have some extra days, so I know it won't be a problem time wise. What do you think? Would that be okay with you? You don't have to answer now, just think about it and let me know after the Sabbath."

"Oh, no thinking required on that one. That would be wonderful. With your help in a few days, you could do more than I could do in a year." Amos sounded truly excited and Timothy too was pleased that he could help and work in the gardens.

"Well my dear, I've finished cleaning up the kitchen." Fi said as she came in the living room.

"Yes, dear. Alright Timothy, you have done more to wear me out today than you know. I think we're headed in for an early night. Please make yourself at home. We have books on the shelf here if you wish to stay up and read."

"Thank you, but I think I'll call it a night too. I didn't sleep well last night the ground was so hard, so I think I'll enjoy the comforts of a bed tonight."

"Okay, suit yourself. Tomorrow will be a relaxing day. Feel free to sleep in, we do. We don't do much on the Sabbath, resting is so luxurious. It's my favorite day!"

His wife gave him a little slap as she shook her head, "Lazy man, come on. Have a good night, Timothy."

"Good night." Timothy followed them down the short hallway, turning into his room. He closed the door and readied for bed. He was indeed tired. He had walked quite a distance in the last three days, plus the lack of sleep and the work from the afternoon. Sleep sounded so good. Knowing that he was welcome to stay for a few days and work on the land pleased him and helped sleep to come quickly for him. His last thought as he drifted off to sleep was how strange it felt not to have the little lamb beside him, he hoped it was okay.

Chapter 10

Timothy slept well through the morning hours, catching up on the rest that he had missed the night before. The dark green curtains helped keep the sunlight out, which meant he slept longer than he normally did. When he awoke he momentarily forgot where he was. Taking a slow look around helped him to remember. He also remembered that it was the Sabbath. He slowly stretched and wondered what time it was. Would they have a worship time together like he did at home? Timothy felt obligated to be a part of it. He had been to one every Sabbath for as long as he could remember, it didn't seem quite right not having a time together. He listened carefully for signs of anyone else being up, but he didn't hear any. "Hmm, they must still be sleeping, or I missed them and they stepped out for a while."

Timothy slowly rose and walked toward the window. He pulled back the green curtains and peered through the dusty glass. The contrast of the dark green curtain (though slightly faded from the sun) compared to the forest outside was drastic. It startled him. "Funny, how you get used to seeing things so green and alive. I never knew that anywhere could be so different. I guess my love for plants really helps make a difference on our property." Timothy whispered to himself. "I hope I can help him see some of that beauty here."

Since there were no other noises in the house, Timothy decided he would quietly go check on his lamb. Maybe Amos and Fi preferred no one joining in their worship time, or perhaps they went up to his grandfather's little cottage and had a service up there and since he slept so long he missed it. "Oh well," he thought, "it can't hurt to miss just one, my first one in 85 years. I suppose I'll take time next week."

Slipping into the barn he headed for the lamb. It was standing there, looking up, waiting expectantly for him. "I guess you knew I'd come. Shall we go for a little walk? We can't go far, maybe to the south side of the pond." He opened the gate and headed out the door, the lamb following right behind him.

The day continued in a very leisurely fashion. Not once did Timothy hear Amos or his wife. He expected they took the Sabbath to the extreme, resting the entire day. It felt a bit awkward at first, but Timothy ended up helping himself to some food in the kitchen. After lunch he decided another nap wasn't such a bad thing and went to lie down. He stirred later when he heard some movement around the house. He decided to get up and see what was happening.

Amos and Fi were in the kitchen talking in hushed tones when Timothy entered. "Hi, Timothy," said Fi, "did you rest well?"

"I did thank you. How about yourself?"

"We did, like I said, I take the day of rest literally," Amos responded with a grin.

"Dinner's almost ready, why don't you two men have a seat. You can make plans for tomorrow. That way Amos will be well rested up for the work you'll make him do, Timothy." She turned with a grin back to the stove.

"I need to go check on my lamb real quick, shall we walk and talk?"

"I have a feeling I'll need all the strength I can save up for tomorrow. I think I'll stay here, thanks."

"Okay," Timothy responded and was off to the pond. When he arrived he began looking around to see if his lamb was anywhere. He didn't see him on the south side, so began walking north around the east side. The sun was setting and as Amos had noted, the reflection in the pond was brilliant. It made up for all the browns as vibrant orange reflected off of everything. Off in the distance Timothy noticed the cabin. There was a man sitting on the porch taking in the scene. Timothy waved and nodded his head. He figured this must be Amos' grandfather. The man returned the nod, but then suddenly rose and went inside the house. Timothy turned and continued looking around until he found his lamb. He took him back to the barn for the night.

Amos, Fi, and Timothy ate their meal together, discussed their plan of action for the next day and then headed to bed. They decided to get an early start on the garden in the morning.

The next day was full of work and more work. Timothy focused on the largest garden. He watered it and elevated some of the leaves and vines in the field. He figured that even though it was late in the season they still might be able to do a little more growing before they were harvested.

On the second day Timothy asked to see the orchard. It was nearly harvest time for the fruit and he wanted to see how Amos' trees were progressing. Timothy was not prepared for what met him in the field. Tall brown weeds grew between the trees. It was about the only healthy thing growing on Amos' property. The trees were all poorly shaped with little leaves that seemed burned by the sun. They looked as if they hadn't ever been pruned. Upon a closer inspection the fruit on nearly every tree was tiny and hard, if it had any fruit on it at all. It wasn't worth picking let alone eating. It would be a waste of time to work in the orchard at this point.

"When was the last time you had a harvest of fruit?" Timothy inquired.

"Oh, I don't know, maybe about 20 years ago or so. It was a couple of years after my father left. I don't normally even bother coming out here to check any more. We had a goat at one time, he did a decent job at keeping the grass around here short, but lately we haven't needed him so I gave him to another family."

Timothy noticed that his voice trailed off. That was the second time he'd mentioned something about his father. Didn't he say when he came that there were only three of them that lived on this territory? That didn't seem normal. Most families had dozens of people living on their land, like their own little community. It did make one wonder what happened to the rest of Amos' family.

"Trees need to be trimmed in the spring time, before they begin their growth in order to produce a better harvest. Now would not do them any good." Timothy looked around as they continued walking through the small orchard. "Where is your main pond? Is it on this side of your land?" he questioned.

"No, the pond on the west side is all we have. It's low this year, but it does the job. We also have a well close to our house and one close to my grandfather's house."

"Yes, I've noticed it. Does your grandfather ever come out and help in the garden, or is that not his thing either?"

"He used to. He and my father were the main caretakers. But he doesn't anymore."

Timothy's curiosity was raised. He wasn't sure if it would be a welcome question, but he had to ask. "Do you mind if I ask where your father is?"

"Don't know. He left one year, much like you are doing, with a lamb to sacrifice in Jerusalem. Our land looked much better than, but then again, he was a natural gardener. He never came back."

"So you never heard from him again. No message at all. Do you even know if he made it to Jerusalem?"

"I haven't any idea. It was his first year going, taking my grandfather's place. Maybe he didn't know the way. Maybe he got lost, I don't know. My mother was so upset that she left a few years later. She has never returned either. So it remains my grandfather, my wife and I. We are simple people, we don't have a lot and we don't expect much, we just live on our land and that is all." His voice sounded so monotone, like he didn't care or it didn't matter or he really couldn't change it so why bother.

Timothy was puzzled at this information. Why would his father never come back, especially if he had loved the land and gardening? What was it that caused him to not return? Surely it couldn't be that he got lost; there were many people willing to help show the way. How could the land waste away so quickly in such a short period of time?

There was no question that the land needed a lot of work. Rather than pondering on questions that could not be answered, Timothy decided to pour himself into the land, willing it to live and grow through his care. He focused solely on the garden for the better part of the week. He rose before the sun came up and stayed out long after it had disappeared. Each day he made sure the soil was cultivated and watered. He wanted the crops to improve for Amos and his wife. He wanted the crops to improve because of all of his hard work. He wanted to show just how amazing gardens could look.

As the week progressed Amos' wife seemed a little more perturbed. Timothy had heard some angry whispering one night as he lay in his bed.

"There isn't that much food! There's barely enough for the three of us, let alone some stranger who decides to stay on indefinitely!"

"But look how hard Timothy is working. He is working his hardest to produce a better crop for us."

"But, the truth of the matter is that it isn't going to drastically improve our crop for this year. He's come too late!" Fi spat at him in her hoarse whisper. "The harvest time has come, growing season is over! We can't continue to give our food to this man; we need it to survive for the rest of this year. He will have to leave!"

Amos did not agree. "We'll scrape by this year, you'll see. The improvements will be well worth it in the end. If you would just come out to the fields and see what is happening you'd know."

"I know now! I don't have to leave this house and look at that dry dirt for you to tell me our crop is going to be great, because it isn't! Face it Amos, it's not making that much of a difference!"

Timothy wished that she would go check on their work. He had seen some progress, at least the leaves looked a little brighter, that should mean some growth in the plant, but you really couldn't tell until you harvested them. But she wouldn't go, so what did it matter? She refused to leave the house. Even going as far as the well outside was too far for her. She would much rather stay in their drab little house and do her housework than see the dullness of the outdoors.

Timothy felt that his time working had been profitable. If he could just stay long enough to till the other gardens it would be such a benefit for next year. He knew he could get his hands on some seeds and that would be so helpful to Amos and his wife, as long as he would daily check his gardens and make sure they had an adequate water supply. Otherwise, he would be in about the same predicament, or worse next year.

One morning, the tension in the air was too thick for Timothy. He decided to skip breakfast and go for a walk instead. As he walked he realized that he hadn't seen the little lamb in a while. He had been neglecting it and he wasn't exactly sure how it was fairing. The gardens had simply consumed all of his time. This realization gave him a start and some concern as to the whereabouts and the status of his little charge. After all, he wasn't an entirely irresponsible person, even though it wasn't a job on the top of his list.

As he walked toward the pond, the reflection of the sun rising over it captured his attention. He stood there for a moment before he glanced over at the little shack and noticed that his lamb was on the porch with Amos' grandfather. Timothy decided to approach the man. He had not yet spoken to him, even though he'd been there for nearly a week. Amos' grandfather was intent on rubbing the lamb's ears and seemed to be talking to it.

"Ah, little lamb. You are worth so much. Do people realize your great significance? I think not, they brush you aside as if you were a common item that didn't need attention. Oh how little they know. You and I know don't we. This isn't how it should be."

"Good morning," Timothy said quietly as he approached the front porch. "I'm Timothy, I've been staying with Amos and Fi."

"Yep, I know. Been watchin' you. You work hard. Love those fields don't you boy?"

"There's nothing better than getting into the soil and seeing the labor of your work grow from day to day."

"Oh really?" the man responded, his voice rising, "nothing better?"

Quest for a True Heart

In an instant Timothy felt like he had been caught. The truth was not hidden from this man. Although they had never spoken his gaze held a knowing look, a look that told him he knew the truth, he knew Timothy would rather stay here and work then travel on to Jerusalem.

Timothy wouldn't admit that that thought had crossed his mind more than once. What would it be for him to stay here for a year or so? His family would never know. He could leave the lamb, work on the fields here and have them producing well in no time. Amos' family would be far better off for it (Amos needed all the help and encouragement he could get) and his family, well, his family had plenty of hands to carry on the work there. They wouldn't miss him.

"Sit down boy." Timothy obeyed taking the other empty chair on the porch. He had a feeling he was going to hear this man's opinion. The man rubbed the lamb's ears one more time before he leaned back in his chair and looked out over the pond with its bouncing orange reflections.

"You know boy, this place didn't always look this way."

"Yes sir, Amos told me that it was better about 20 years ago, when you cared for it. He said that he doesn't have much of a mind for the field and has let it go downhill."

"Oh, is that what he says?"

Timothy nodded in response.

"Well, that shows how little he knows. It has nothing to do with his lack of care or his laziness. He could work from sun up to sun down like you and it would still look the same. You know, you're wasting your time boy. This isn't where you are supposed to be. This is not God's will for you."

Timothy shifted in his chair. He was beginning to feel really uncomfortable. He knew it was a strain on Amos and Fi for him to be here, but he thought the benefits would far outweigh what he would eat and the stress of low food amounts now. What was this man talking about? How could God not want him here, to help?

"Did Amos tell you about his father?"

"He said he left 20 years ago to offer a sacrifice in Jerusalem. He said he never came back, didn't know what happened."

"Yea, that's about right. I sent my son on his first trip to Jerusalem to offer a sacrifice 20 years ago. Thought he was ready to be head of the family. He was my only son. My dear wife and I only ever had one child, but we raised him to fear God. Didn't know until it was too late that he had no regard for God or the lives we lived. He'd been pretending all the while and when he was asked to do something he didn't want to and couldn't do appropriately he ran. Took off. It's my fault you know. I should have known he wasn't ready to go. I should have listened more and prayed. Now, no one in our family goes to Jerusalem. Amos is complacent about worshipping God. I guess his father never taught him it was important, so he doesn't feel that it's important either. I'm sure you noticed how his Sabbath lacked some serious praise? He just doesn't care to admit that he owes gratitude and a few other things to God. I've stayed up here, hounding myself for years about the choices I've made. I simply can't forgive or undo what has been done. I can't figure it out. What was it that I didn't show them? How come they don't understand? What else could I have done? I've been praying ever since, begging God's forgiveness and mercy, but all we're left with is this little forsaken piece of land, that continually gets worse each year. We haven't had rain in many years. The land cannot survive much longer and neither can we. Especially not with you draining what is left of this little pond into the garden. It won't help. It will only mean no more water for us to drink. Then we will go faster. No, what's done here is my fault and there isn't any way you can fix it. You need to get your stuff together and take your lamb and leave, the sooner the better for us and for you. You don't need to be causing the same trouble for your family."

Timothy couldn't believe it. All this simply because their family wasn't represented in Jerusalem, not from laziness and lack of work; a beautiful land destroyed because one person wouldn't or couldn't offer a sacrifice with a true heart to God. Could it really be true? Perhaps him leaving wasn't such a bad idea, but not to Jerusalem. He should go home and tell his father to go to Jerusalem for him, that way their land would be saved. He could never offer this lamb worthily. He hadn't even remembered his lamb this week, too caught up was he in working the land and fooling himself that he was making improvements. According to what he just heard the only improvement he was making was drying up the land of the last bit of water that was left in the pond, the one thing that allowed them to survive and would continue to allow them to survive for a little bit longer if it were left alone.

Why hadn't he seen the signs before? He had been warned numerous times by his grandfather. It was all there, he knew it. He just hadn't believed it to be more than words before today.

The land lacked vibrancy, the trees around this property plainly told of a water shortage. They were barely surviving themselves, let alone this man and his territory. Without rain, one couldn't survive on their land. What was Timothy to do? Was it really true that all of his natural ability in the garden, all of his effort was pointless? Did he really lack the gardening talent and ability that he had boasted about?

He excused himself from Amos' grandfather and headed for the orchard. He needed to think, to clear his thoughts. He needed to know the truth. He had to believe for himself if what he had been taught his entire life was fact and if this man was indeed telling the truth, that the land looked as it did due to a lack of blessing, not a lack of work.

The orchard at home was his favorite place, his place of comfort and peace, the place he would go to find his answers or just to get away from everyone. It was the place he needed to go now, to walk through and to talk. When he arrived he received yet another reminder of what no rain and no care did to a place. 'The goat was no longer needed to keep the grass cut.' He remembered Amos telling him the first time he'd come out here. Of course, looking at the grass now, it was dead, fallen over, it blended into the hard packed earth. The trees with their wild branches looked sick. It was like the pain in his stomach, nauseating. All of this, because of a fake heart, because he said he believed and wouldn't tell his father the truth. Or was it because he never went to Jerusalem? What happened to him in Jerusalem? Surely the King would know the intentions of his heart. Had he gotten rid of him?

Knowing the truth, offering a sacrifice, and coming back to face reality wasn't something that Amos' father must have been able to handle. He couldn't, so instead, he must have chosen never to return and to leave his father and son to suffer the consequences. Never really knowing how or if they would survive.

Timothy's thoughts wandered to Amos' grandfather. For 20 years he sat in his home, blaming himself for what happened, but never taking any action to right the wrong. For 20 years he and his grandson suffered. Would it end in death? Could these people really die because of a simple act of disobedience? That sounded to extreme for Timothy. Surely God wouldn't allow such devastation if Amos' grandfather still loved Him. And what could this mean for his own family?

Timothy heard a rustle from around one of the trees that disturbed his thinking. He turned and saw Ross standing next to a barren, withered fig tree. "How much is your orchard worth to you, Timothy? You know it's not you and all your hard work that make it look so full and prosperous. It has been your father's and your grandfather's and your great grandfather's worship over the years that has made the difference. Their true hearts are the ones that have kept Aarde Daal looking the way it does today. They know, they have seen, and they believe. God is true and only He is worthy of worship, not the trees, grass and plants. It is to him that you owe your work, your all, your life, your praise and your sacrifice. Are you ready to quit hiding here and stop relying on your own strength and wisdom and start heading northeast like you are supposed to? Are you ready to follow God's plan? You take the next step and God will come through. Trust Him, it's not as hard as you think. He knows your heart, he sees your efforts. Stop fooling yourself by thinking you are making a difference here. Start realizing it is He who makes all the difference. It is He whom you need to recognize."

"But what if," Timothy wasn't given the chance to finish, Ross was gone. "Just go? God sees my heart." Timothy muttered. "If he sees my heart, He'll know it doesn't match my feet, Ross." Timothy hollered out as he kicked the dry ground. "Some friend you are! I thought you were supposed to guide, lead, make sure we stay faithful to God. How are you fulfilling God's purpose by just saying what you think and then leaving?"

It was a frustrated Timothy that headed back to the main house. He had trudged around for most of the morning, trying to sort out his thoughts. Comments from Amos' grandfather and Ross continued to echo back and forth in his mind. He had a feeling he knew what he needed to do, however, his heart was filled with more dread over that choice than the alternative. Who said the harder road was the better road anyway? What if it didn't work out or worse even ended up like Jacan even if he went?

When he finally arrived at the house neither Amos nor Fi were anywhere in sight. He thought he'd head to the barn. Amos was inside getting some tools for the day's work.

"There you are. And here I thought you were the early morning worker." He chuckled a bit, "Look, I'm even out here getting ready to work before you." He paused as he picked up a tool then continued. "Fi and I were just talking about you. You know you have been such a blessing here to me this past week. You know how to take care of the vegetation. It has never been my strong suit. And it is looking so much better under your care already. I can tell by the leaves, their color is brighter and they look stronger. I know we can do so much more together. I like working with you. You motivate me and make me want to do better. I think we make a great team. You can teach me what you know about growing and planting and harvesting and everything. Little by little, as I gain knowledge I can take this land back and this here property can be improved. There might just be hope for this place yet. Why don't you just plan to stay here? You could really help me out. I'll give you free reign to make all the choices concerning the plants that you want. You'd be the head decision maker as far as the vegetation is concerned. I bet you could make this place look as good as the "Garden of Eden". What do you say? Wanna stay?"

Timothy paused before responding. The words of Amos' grandfather still echoed in his head, 'It has nothing to do with his lack of care or his laziness. He could work from sun up to sun down like you and it would still look the same.' Would he really be wasting his time as he was told, or was there a real possibility it was just laziness. Did his grandfather really know what he was talking about? Was it a lack of God's blessing?

Timothy knew from experience that elders and resurrected saints knew more and were to be respected. If Amos' grandfather said that it was from lack of representation, then there wasn't any way this land could be fixed until that representation was fixed. No point in trying to cure the symptoms instead of getting right at the cause of the problem.

He had already thought through his many options and he didn't want to make any poor decisions, but he figured it was best to listen to Amos' grandfather and Ross. They had experienced so much more and knew what they were talking about. Plus, they both had true hearts, hearts for serving God, he wasn't so sure that he did. He also knew what the rest of his family would say, plus, his conscience was bothering him as well.

"Hey, why don't you take the night to think about it," Amos chuckled. "It's not like I'm going to kick you out tomorrow or tie you down so you can't leave. Like I said, I think we make a great team you and me. I think we could turn this place around in no time and really show these people how to garden. Who knows, you could be a hero, famous! You'd be known as the man who could restore land, command life to come back from the dead. Why, people would be coming from all around to ask your advice. You might even get to travel worldwide then. See these different lands and their vegetation. Rescue their land like this one and learn about new species of plants. I mean think of all the varieties that must be out there."

Amos' comments caused Timothy to pause again. 'Land, travel, different varieties of plants, such richness and possibility,' he thought. Dare he consider? Then Timothy's stomach rumbled and he remembered the reason he'd missed breakfast. "What about your wife?"

"Oh, don't worry about her. We'll win her over. You'll see. She'll be our first convert and probably your greatest supporter. She really does like having you around, she just worries, that's all. She might even be willing to be your manager when you make it big. She's really a great organizer."

His mind was still spinning from these new possibilities. "Be famous? Me?" he chuckled, "People come to me to heal their lands. I'd be like… I'd be like…the Master Restorer. Hmm," Timothy thought. The thought had its appeal.

"Look, like I said, I don't need an answer right now, just think about it and let me know. Come on, let's get to work."

With that the two of them headed for the garden, Timothy with his thoughts full of confusing and contradicting words and Amos with a spring in his step for the first time because he finally felt like he was getting on top of his struggles.

Chapter 11

They worked hard all day and decided to call it quits early that night as they were both worn out and Timothy still had a lot of thinking to do.

"I'm headed to bed. It's been a long, tiring day. I'll see you in the morning. We can talk more then. I know you've got a lot to think about. You've been distracted all day. Good night."

"Good night."

Timothy stood mesmerized as he watched Amos head down the hallway, it felt like hours had passed, but it was really mere seconds. Why, he sure had something to chew on tonight. What would he do? The truth was, he was enjoying this, being with Amos and working on his land. He had a friend, someone who understood him and was willing to listen to him ramble on about plants and different methods and theories about farming. But, he didn't want to let his family down either.

Timothy meandered around the house thinking, until he noticed that he had wandered into the living room beside a shelf of books. The one Fi had pointed out the first night, but he had never made it to it because he had been so busy and tired from working so hard. He decided he would take advantage of the quiet living room tonight. He knew he wasn't going to be able to go to sleep yet. He had too much thinking to do. He plopped himself into the chair nearest the bookshelf, just opposite the window.

His rocking started slowly, like his thoughts, as he stared in the direction of the window without really seeing it. "What will I do? What should I do?" he mumbled half to himself and half to the empty room. "Could you imagine, people coming to me from all over the world to ask my advice about their plants. They'd probably pay in plants, which would give me so many varieties. I could open a museum of sorts, a plant garden and people would come from around the world to see me and buy an assortment of plants from me or ask me advice." Could he make this work? Maybe just maybe. His heart started pounding quickly at the thought. That was what he lived for, plants, growing things. He would feel so fulfilled, worthwhile and alive. He would feel like he had a purpose, that what he was doing was important.

"But then, there is my family. What will they suffer if I don't go to Jerusalem, and don't offer a sacrifice?" Maybe he could send word to them to let them know that his plans had changed. He wouldn't desert them as Amos' father had. His dad could go in his place, there was still time. It would have been way better that way in the first place. His dad's heart was far more dedicated to God than his was. Then he would be free to stay and work. But, could he make a difference? Amos' grandfather didn't seem to think so, neither did Ross. This was God's doing and no amount of work was going to fix it without hearts being fixed and dedication and praise being given to God, or so they said.

Timothy's gaze shifted from the direction of the window to rest of the room. It really was a simple home. There was a faded, little couch, a worn chair, a small, scuffed up wooden table and an old wooden shelf of books built into the wall beside the window. The books looked as if they hadn't been disturbed for quite some time. His eyes glanced across the spines while casually reading the titles. Nothing really struck his fancy. They

Quest for a True Heart

didn't have anything on gardening. Then he noticed the book on the end of the shelf. <u>Having God's Heart</u>, "Hmmm," Timothy thought, "interesting."

He stopped rocking and reached over to remove it from the shelf. The book looked as if it had never been opened before, let alone read. He opened the cover and looked at the first page, it read, "It's a terrifying thing to fall into the hands of the living God. Hebrews 10:31 Please, follow your instructions. R.S. John."

Timothy knew what R.S. stood for, that was how Ross always signed his name too, Resurrected Saint. The pieces of the puzzle were quickly fitting together. And they didn't seem to be adding up in his favor. It was no accident that this man's crops were failing, or that the watering hole was no longer sufficient to water his crops. It wasn't laziness either. Amos' grandfather had to be right. Timothy also figured that it wasn't the neighbors that had so much need for the other animals, such as the goat he gave away, as it was that this man and his wife were no longer able to care and feed them. It was then that he remembered the statement from their first meeting, "I never did see reason why one should wear themselves out each year on such a long journey." Timothy began to put together when this family had a representative last go to Jerusalem to celebrate the Feast of Booths and when the fields had begun their deterioration. Perhaps Amos' dad had never made it to Jerusalem. So why hadn't his grandfather gone again, or worked with Amos to teach him and guide him in going? Surely he wasn't lazy in every area. He must have to care about something.

A shudder ran down Timothy's back. What if his family's farm turned out this way because he worshipped unworthily or not at all? His lush farm, his beautiful fields, the large pond, turned to dust? The thought did more than scare him, it made him sick to his stomach. But Ross had told him to go, assured him or started to, that this was the best plan of action. Ross didn't tell him to turn back and get his dad, but instead to get up and keep moving forward.

He turned back to the book, <u>Having God's Heart</u>. Perhaps he needed this book just as much as the man of this house did. Maybe this would make the going forward a lot easier. Timothy sat back in the chair, propped up his legs and began to read.

Chapter 12

"Chapter 1 – Where is God? Please write down where God is."

"What? Timothy flipped through the first chapter. All the pages were blank, nothing. There were about 10 pages with absolutely nothing on them, not on the front and not on the back. He held the book closer to the light to see if the writing had faded, but from what he could tell, there had never been any writing.

"What is this? A workbook?" He flipped back to the first page. "Where is God? *Where is God?* Well, He's in Jerusalem, where else?" Timothy didn't understand. Why would there be so many blank pages? The question wasn't that difficult. He flipped to the back of the chapter, carefully looking over each page.

On the bottom of the last page was written, "There are many places that you can find God, in many things. Everything on earth tells something about God and His character. There would be too many to write them all down, but if you have filled in these pages in chapter one, then you are

Quest for a True Heart

ready to move on to chapter 2. You may turn the page. If you have not filled in chapter 1 completely, please do NOT move ahead, you still have much work to do before your heart his ready."

Timothy closed the book and examined it. The book looked like it had been sitting on the shelf for quite some time. It appeared not to have been given any attention. He wondered if this book had been given to Amos or to Amos' father before he left for Jerusalem. He guessed that his resurrected saint must have tried to warn him. If that was the case then Amos really did know the reason the land looked like this, but if it was for his father, perhaps then Amos didn't know as much as he should, but you would think with the book being on his shelf he would have taken some notice. Then again, he wasn't exactly the go getter type. "Why then hasn't your grandfather said anything?" Timothy mumbled to himself.

Time passed slowly until Timothy made a decision. He decided that what happened here to Amos' land was NOT what he wanted to happen to his land at home, or really his family's land. If Amos wasn't going to use this book to get himself back on the right track then Timothy figured he could. Fi had said to make himself at home.

He picked up a pencil that had been lying on the end table, opened to the first page of chapter 1 and wrote down 'Jerusalem.'

"Where else could they mean? 'Heaven', 'Zion', 'the Celestial city'. How many more names for Zion could there be?" Timothy flipped back to the end of the chapter and read the note again. "'Everything on earth tells something about God and His character.' Everything, eh?" he continued. "Hmm..." With that Timothy started to think about his life.

His father, his grandfather, his great grandfather, obviously all had some similar traits, they loved to sing and talk about God, so God could be seen in them. Ross and other Resurrected Saints definitely had God's character in them because they got to spend time worshipping Him and spreading His love around. As he listed his family members and the resurrected saints he knew, he filled up the first page. "Who or what else? Where is God?"

At that moment the wind gusted outside causing Timothy to look out the window. It moved the tree's branches, stirred up the dirt and whistled past the house. Wasn't there a story that his grandfather used to tell him about God's voice being in the wind? It had something to do with a prophet who wanted to know where God was after he had faced his enemy and he was in a cave. God had sent a strong wind, an earthquake and a fire, but He had been in neither one of those, He did appear in a gentle, blowing wind.

"Wind, I can write that." And he did. "Well, if He's in the wind, He could be in other things too. I suppose since Elijah expected him to be in the strong wind, earthquake and fire He could have been in those." Timothy wrote all of them down and continued to list things around him and things from his past. It wasn't that these things were God, but because He created them they revealed things about Himself.

It wasn't until he was on the third page that he thought of plants, fruit, and trees. He also listed every person in his community that he could think of who was really close to God and Bahaudeen and his family too.

After some careful thinking and the passing of a good portion of the evening Timothy had managed to fill up the pages. As he neared the end he looked back to review what he had written. His family members and members of the community, the resurrected saints, and then came the list of plants, animals, and other creation's of God. He tried to also name a number of places, but since he had never left Aarde Daal, he couldn't elaborate on that point. It was as he was perusing the list of plants that he realized how much he had really written. God was everywhere and a part of everything. Why he had not noticed this before came as a shock to him. He wasn't just in the words and actions of his family, but He was also in everything that Timothy worked with on a daily basis. The leaves, the roots, the stems, all supported the plant to help it live as God supported this earth. His great grandfather had told him about the evil in the earth before, but he never understood it, however he was beginning to understand it now. The earth was good and so beautiful now, because God was in it and ruled over it. He was everywhere, unlike what it had been before He had come to reign on earth. When Timothy compared his land and Amos' land he could definitely see that when God was praised, given recognition, and was allowed to be a part of the land, He was what made it good, not just human work. He was what made things support life and grow, He was the life. What if Timothy took the route that Amos had taken and instead of asking his grandfather why the changes had come to the land, had just been satisfied with not recognizing God, being lazy and doing nothing about it. What would the outcome for the rest of his family be then?

Timothy turned to the last page having one more blank to fill in. He carefully wrote his name, Timothy Steade. "Yes," whispered Timothy, "even though I have not seen or have chosen not to see, God is in me. He is with me. He chooses to be with me."

Now Timothy knew that he could turn the page to the second chapter. He did so with anticipation, knowing that God was with him and was going to make all the difference on this journey and in his life. Being sure he was worthy or had a true heart was another matter, but he was ready to deal with one step at a time for now.

Chapter 2 started with the title "Following God." Timothy slouched down into the chair, not realizing the time as it passed. He read on, learning how God loved him and how it wasn't just an action that you did to follow God, it was an emotion that you felt. Sometimes though that emotion could be hidden and then it would seem as though nothing were there. That was when it was most important to follow God, to continue the action of following Him, whether you felt like it or not, for when you continued to do so, only then would you understand God, and then the feelings would come.

Timothy read on, the pages seeming to turn themselves. He read some of the history of the world, how it was created and how God desired a relationship with the people He created on the earth. He was so desperate to guide those that He willing sent people to give up their lives to lead the way. When that wasn't enough He sent His Son, His only Son. Timothy reading the facts for the first time without his family seemed to make the story feel more realistic to him. It wasn't just a part of them it was a real event that really occurred, because the God who made him cared. The fact was, it happened, it wasn't just something his territory believed. It was a worldwide truth.

Timothy turned and read the last chapter's title, "True Worship". This was the chapter he needed. With all of the history that had been presented and the revelation of how much this God sacrificed for him he knew worship was his expected response. He also knew that if he could not worship in a worthy manner it would mean all kinds of trouble for him and his family.

"Worship," he read in anticipation, somehow he knew this chapter was going to change everything, or at least he hoped it would. He scooted out toward the edge of his seat, bending over the book, fully absorbed in its final pages. "Worship is walking." He read. "What? Worship is walking, what does that mean? If worship was really walking then just the walk there would be sufficient, I shouldn't need a little lamb or anything else. If walking were really worship I could do that around the fields, especially here!" He shook his head as he read on, "Worship is an activity that God wants you and I to participate in. It demands a heart response, not passive, but an active, participative response.[116]"

He read on about the story of Abraham in Genesis 22 where he went to sacrifice his son Isaac. What would be considered a horrible thing, something that Timothy had never heard of happening before, had been asked by God of Abraham, he was to kill his beloved son. God considered this worship. The fact that Abraham got up and intended to do this horrendous deed was thought to be worship, because it was obedience. "Somehow, these terrible, unexplainable, disagreeable moments are right because it is what God has asked of us. He asks for total surrender. Surrender of intellect, emotion, and will. We are to give up what we believe is right and act on what we know God has asked us to do. This ACTION, is worship."

Timothy's heart felt like it had dropped into his stomach. He had stopped walking, he had stopped worshipping. Even though he didn't feel as though he were worthy to sacrifice in Jerusalem, nor did he feel full or praise, and even though he didn't really want to do it, the mere fact that he was walking there and planning on doing it was a form of worship. It was the initial action required to get the ultimate goal. It was the obedience that the King was looking for.

As Timothy finished the last page he closed the book. The sun was just beginning to rise. He could see the orangey red glow over the trees. It was going to be a beautiful day, a perfect day for being outside. Timothy knew without hesitation that he would be leaving and walking to Jerusalem. He didn't know what was in store, but he knew he had to bring his sacrificial lamb and offer it to the King of Kings on behalf of his family. He trusted that God would see his efforts and obedience and change his heart, he knew, he had to go. He glanced at the last line in the book before closing it, putting it in his memory, "Worship demands a response, make it from your heart."

Chapter 13

It took little time for Timothy to gather his few belongings and write a farewell note. No amount of persuasion could change his mind at this moment. Although he was thankful that it was still early enough that Amos and Fi were asleep, he really didn't want to explain the book to him, nor his thinking. He knew he couldn't convince Amos and he was afraid he would talk himself out of going because he wasn't worthy. No, he would go, if for no other reason than the benefit of his family and the saving of his land, or for simply walking in obedience, he had to be on his way. He did want to know more about this God and why He would require such sacrifices as a lamb. It was no longer just because his family was filled with Him, but because He had offered such a great sacrifice for Timothy. Imagine, He gave up his Son, His only Son, so that this world could exist. So that Timothy could live in the peaceful world that he knew with all of the blessings. The least Timothy could do was find out why and give a little of himself, like giving up his harvest time to travel. He quietly placed the card on the table and slipped out the door. He knew he needed to get going.

Timothy went to the barn to get his lamb. His mind last night had been buzzing with possibilities and thoughts. When he reached the barn he realized that he hadn't taken the time to lock up his lamb. Actually, he hadn't taken much time the entire week to check on his lamb. He remembered seeing it with Amos' grandfather last night and decided it was probably around there.

Timothy headed toward the pond. "I hope it's still there?" he thought.

As Timothy neared Amos' grandfather's cabin he saw some movement. The man was opening up the front door. There in his arms was the little lamb. He looked comfortable and secure in the man's arms, as if he enjoyed his new caretaker. A pang of jealousy hit Timothy hard. He had never experienced such a feeling before. Before the jealous root had time to grow, his humility overrode it[117]. The lamb deserved better care. He had not been careful. It served him right if the lamb did not wish to follow him anymore, or if the man did not wish to give him up. Perhaps that was his only comfort on this forsaken land.

"I saw this little lamb outside. He looked so lost and lonely that I tried to coax him in last night. Funny little thing, he wouldn't come in. It took me most of the night before he would enter and when he did he stayed right by the door. He's a smart little fellow he knows who his true shepherd is. I hope that you've come back to take on your rightful responsibility," he said as he put the lamb down on the porch.

"Yes sir, I do intend to take this little lamb today and head toward Jerusalem. I've left a note explaining...." He trailed off, then paused and restarted more confidently, "It is time I go. Thank you for trying to care for this lamb. I'll do much better in the future, I promise. I uh," Timothy paused again for a moment, "I, uh… thank you for your words the other day. They were very helpful. I needed to hear them."

"Humph," he grumbled and nodded his head, as if to say 'Get going.'

"Come," Timothy said, as the lamb rose to follow, "We'll be on our way then." He picked up the lamb and made it comfortable in his arms. It felt right. It felt secure. With his pack on and water in his canteen Timothy started down the road. Love for the creature began to grow in him as he stroked his little head. He didn't bother to look back. His mind was in one direction, the same direction as his feet. He needed to make up for lost time and get to Jerusalem. He had one day of travel before the Sabbath again and as far as Timothy was concerned he wanted to get as much space as he could between Jacan and him.

Chapter 14

By midmorning Timothy was well into the woods, past the stark, drab trees and into more luscious trees, a landscape that he was used to seeing. He hummed as he walked. A song his great grandfather had taught him. He began to sing it for the little lamb and for himself. There was no time like the present to start working on his attitude and his praise for this journey. He had been lax for far too long.

> "O worship the King, all glorious above,
> O gratefully sing God's power and God's love;
> Our Shield and Defender, the Ancient of Days,
> Pavilioned in splendor, and girded with praise.
>
> O tell of God's might, O sing of God's grace,
> Whose robe is the light, whose canopy space,
> Whose chariots of wrath the deep thunderclouds form,

And dark is God's path on the wings of the storm.

Thy bountiful care, what tongue can recite?
It breathes in the air, it shines in the light;
It streams from the hills, it descends to the plain,
And sweetly distills in the dew and the rain.

O measureless Might, ineffable Love,
While angels delight to hymn you above.
The humbler creation, though feeble their lays,
With true adoration shall sing to your praise.[118]"

The words lifted his spirits some as he walked. Memories of his family singing as well as the words themselves helped to encourage his burdened heart. He knew that he was on the right path.

He contemplated the words of the song as he walked. Some he understood, like God being the Ancient of Days or having a white robe, some he thought might make more sense once he'd been to Jerusalem, like being pavilioned in splendor, and some he didn't think he would ever understand like the chariots of wrath and thunderclouds or storms.

He remembered his great grandfather saying, "*This song was such a comfort to me when things on earth looked like they were coming to an end. When it looked like I couldn't make it one more day. But, through it all I knew God's power would never fail, that He would surely come through for me because I had faith.*" His great grandfather's desire through the entire messy world at that time was to praise God and continue to trust Him. Since then his great grandfather had always praised God and as far as he was concerned he would continue until his last breath.

"I don't get it," Timothy mumbled to the lamb, stroking his head again, "There isn't anything wrong with the earth to need that comfort now, it's all been fixed. Besides, how can a song give you real comfort?"

Although all he had ever seen on earth, up until recently, was peace and prosperity, growth and beauty, seeing Jacan gave him a little more understanding, however he still couldn't completely picture what it would

Quest for a True Heart

be like without God's blessings at all or how it could look much worse than what he saw. But, it was enough for now, enough to show Timothy that God's goodness and grace were present on the earth that he lived on, and that he just hadn't realized it before. He wondered how many other things he had misunderstood because they had been so common place to him.

Timothy's brisk walk continued. He had not slackened his pace all morning. Even though he had been up all night and had not eaten he still kept on. The farther he walked the better the forest started to look. Timothy hoped that if he made it to another settlement tonight it would not be like the one he just left. As it turned out he did not make it to another settlement. This was best, because it allowed him time to think and really dwell on all he had read and discovered. He wished he would have brought the book with him, that way he could refer to it or reread it, especially the parts he was unsure of.

"You seem like you're in a hurry today," Ross commented to him as he kept pace with Timothy. "Something wrong?"

"Oh hi Ross, I just thought it would be best to get going and catch up on some missed time. You know, action is the key to everything. If one doesn't move how can one really tell if they ever intend to?"

"True, good intentions are only intentions until you make a point to make them into actions."

"Yeah, I guess I've decided I needed to change my intentions and maybe learn a few things. Hey, can I ask you a question?"

"Sure."

"Would God really require a life in order to worship Him?"

"Well, can you think of a better gift to offer Him?"

"What do you mean?"

"God created everything. For Him to take care of you, see to your needs, and plan out all your future, do you not think Him deserving of some kind of gift?"

"I guess. So then, a lamb?"

"Yes, a lamb would work. But is that the best thing you could give Him?"

"Well, I guess I could give Him many lambs and oxen and animals. You mean like a larger sacrifice, more animals and bigger animals?"

"I guess that could work, but isn't there something of even greater value that you could give?"

Timothy thought. What else would he give? He knew it had to be an animal, it could not be fruit or vegetables, those things were unacceptable. He was also limited to the kind of animals. He knew his grandfather had been very specific in mentioning which animals could be sacrificed.

"You know, God doesn't want "something" meaning a material thing that you could give Him. He already owns everything. What He wants is you. Yes, He would be willing to accept the many things you have to offer Him as a sacrifice, but remember, you are important to Him."

"Me?"

"Yes, of course. God made you. He wants your worship. It isn't just because God wants to see everyone bowing to Him. He knows that following Him is a far better way of life than anything else you could plan, even your fields. He wants what is best for you, not just for your father or grandfather or even great grandfather because they have served Him. He wants a relationship with each person. To get that relationship He would not ask anything of you that would not be for your benefit."

Timothy thought on those words for a minute before he went to ask another question. "But what if...?" Ross was no longer there, he had left. "He wants me? Why? What about the lamb or my father or grandfather or great grandfather or someone else? Why me? I do not know enough about God. What could I ever do for God?" The questions kept coming, tripping over each other, trying to make some reason or sense with what Ross had said.

It had been a long, draining day. He felt emotionally spent and physically tired. After putting the lamb down to graze on the grass he spread out his blanket and picked some berries and dug up some roots for his dinner. He wasn't overly hungry. He rested his feet in the rippling creek while mindlessly popping berries into his mouth. Leaning on the tree he looked around for the first time and really noticed his surroundings.

Everything was once again beautiful, vibrant, with green colors and, and it was so peaceful. He hadn't even noticed it before, how everything was calm and worked together so effortlessly. He had always just assumed that was the way it was supposed to be, nothing wrong, everything blooming to perfection. Was it really God that was in control of all of it? Had it really been as terrible as his grandfather had described? Or was it worse? Or better? He began to think up all the things his great grandfather had ever told him about earth before.

He remembered the pruning hooks and plowshares, how they had been weapons, things to use for fighting and harming people. "What would that look like?" Timothy thought.

An image slowly began to form in his mind. He imagined vast fields of dead and dry trees and plants, like Jacan, but everywhere. He imagined somber, lazy people who dragged themselves around all day long, not caring. It wasn't fascinating, it was horrifying. People only cared about themselves, what they wanted for the moment, not what was best for everyone. The images became clearer as Timothy lied down for the night. They were so opposite from what he was used to. That night, for the first time that Timothy could remember, he had nightmares. His dreams terrified him. They were not filled with the peace and love that he had become so accustomed too, but with pride, envy and selfishness, the emotions that had begun to sprout within himself.

He awoke in the early morning trembling, feeling around for the little lamb. It lay peacefully beside him, not noticing his terror. Timothy rose to his knees, the feeling of desperation steeling through his body for the first time, like cold ice expanding and freezing his body.

"God," he groaned, "Oh God, I've been so wrong." He moaned again, his head bent low, buried in his blanket. He groped for the tree roots that protruded from the ground, trying to keep his head from swaying; they landed instead on the sleeping lamb. "Oh God, what have I done? I have casually taken all you have given me for granted for my entire life. I didn't know, I didn't realize. I still feel like I don't completely understand. Please, God, please, help me to understand. Help me to be worthy for You." He broke down crying, sobbing, the little lamb peacefully stayed in his place. Finally Timothy fell back to sleep, this time more peacefully.

When he awoke the next morning he felt all broken inside. The faithful lamb was still by his side, trusting in his shepherd and being there for his comfort. Timothy wasn't sure he could fix it, but he knew, from the book, from Ross, from his family, that moving forward was the only way he was going to discover worship, turning back or staying put wasn't an option. He spent the next day setting his mind on his goal, thinking over his plan and what decisions he needed to make. He was determined to make it to Jerusalem, there would be no more stopping now. He would press on, even if he didn't feel like it, he knew that at least his actions were right. Hopefully the desire to continue would come later. Hopefully he would understand more, learn more. Right now he felt like a blind man walking into the unknown, either preparing to face the greatest enemy or the kindest friend, but which he wasn't sure, perhaps it was both.

After a more restful night, he gathered his belongings and took his first steps for the day. His feet felt heavy, but he kept on. His sights were set in one direction.

Meanwhile, in Zion, Tearle saw Ross. "Hey Ross, how was your day?"

"It was okay. I stopped in on Timothy for part of the day. He seems to be doing a bit better, but he still has some struggles. He read that book John left for Amos' father <u>Having God's Heart</u>, it has helped some, but he still has a long way to go. He'll meet up with some friends who will also help, but I want to be sure he sees, understands, and believes the full reality of this journey and God. I know he will feel differently once he arrives in Zion and sees Him face to face, but if he never makes it here or never sets foot in the city, then he will never really know what God is like or what His desires for him are."

"I'll be praying that your time goes well with him. I'll have some of the others pray as well, while we work and prepare. There are some others who have also said they have concerns. This next generation doesn't seem to be as interested in God as the past generations have. They just don't see how magnificent God really is or how much He has done for them."

"Yes, it is hard for them. Having godly parents and grandparents this generation has had an abundance of God's blessing with little effort, but they fail to realize that this blessing will not continue based on their ancestor's actions forever. Once it is their turn to take the lead as heads of these households there will be a decline on this earth and devastation that will be greatly noticed."

"Oh, how terrible. We must organize some extra prayer times and be more diligent about influencing this generation. There must be something extra we can do this year to show these young people God's amazing love and care. For sure, we will keep praying and go before the King to ask this request. He is faithful.[119] I would also be willing to visit Timothy if you think it will help."

"Thanks, he needs it as do many others. I know that God will help us, He has never failed us and He never will. We'll keep in touch and I'll let you know a good time for a visit."

"Sure thing," Tearle responded.

Chapter 15

Early the following morning, when the Sabbath was over, just after daybreak, Timothy was up and ready. He had had enough time to think, and felt like he really needed to get moving, even though his thoughts were still quite jumbled. He trudged on for the better part of the day. He felt as if his brain was clouded and he couldn't see or think clearly. He had questions upon questions, but he knew he would get no answers. All he knew was that he must go forward and forward he went. Step by step he journeyed on, forgetting the importance of plants, forgetting his family, forgetting his surroundings. Ross' words, Jacan and the millions of unanswered questions were buzzing around in his head. The pounding of the questions bouncing back and forth were so loud that they blurred together like a jumbled mass of branches. Timothy didn't even notice the weight of the lamb as he carried it. He had only one goal in mind, get to Jerusalem.

The day began to darken. Timothy knew he needed to stop for dinner and a bite to eat for the lamb. He had travelled quickly all day.

Truly exhausted, almost to the point of not wanting food, Timothy ate a light dinner and then prepared a place to sleep for the night. It did not take him long to have everything situated and the lamb close at his side. He quickly fell into a deep sleep, tired from the emotional turmoil and lack of rest from the past few nights.

When he awoke the next morning he noticed that there was a tiny stream and a few berry bushes nearby, as well as a patch or two of grass for the lamb. It would be sufficient for their breakfast and enough to carry for their lunch as well.

After breakfast and gathering extra fruit, he picked up the lamb and once again started on towards Jerusalem. Today he did not intend to cover as much ground as he did yesterday. He decided to take it at a slower pace and try to see more to the lamb's needs, letting it walk around some and giving it more time to eat.

As he walked he looked down into his shirt pocket and saw a note sticking out. He did not remember putting it there. He pulled it out and looked at the contents.

> "Let not a wise man boast of his wisdom,
> and let not the mighty man boast of his might, let not a rich man boast of his riches; but let him who boasts ***boast of this, that he understands and knows Me***, that I am the LORD who exercises lovingkindness, justice and righteousness on earth; for I delight in these things," declares the LORD.[120]"
> "I am the LORD your God, who **teaches** you to profit, who **leads** you in the way you should go."[121]
> Get to know Him. Let Him be your guide.
>
> -R.S. Ross

"Boast in His understanding, or my understanding of Him." Timothy decided that since he didn't want yesterday's experience of a cloudy mind again he should probably find something with which to occupy it. What would help him know the Lord? How could God teach him? He didn't have any verse books with him, so he decided to try and think of some verses that he had memorized many years ago. He needed something to encourage him, something to help him to feel again, something to keep his mind clear and not be dwelling on what he had almost done. He needed something that would bring him to God. As he thought a section of verses that his great grandfather had repeated on many occasions when he was a boy came to mind. His grandfather had always titled them "About God". Timothy thought he would try and say them.

> "O LORD, You have searched me and known *me*.
> You know when I sit down and when I rise up;
> You understand my thought from afar.

"Oh, what a scary thought, He knows all."

> "You scrutinize my path and my lying down,
> And are intimately acquainted with all my ways.
> Even before there is a word on my tongue,
> Behold, O LORD, You know it all.
> You have enclosed me behind and before,
> And laid Your hand upon me.
> *Such* knowledge is too wonderful for me;

"Too wonderful, to…, He already knows everything, I can do no hiding from Him,

> It is *too* high, I cannot attain to it.
> Where can I go from Your Spirit?
> Or where can I flee from Your presence?
> If I ascend to heaven, You are there;
> If I make my bed in Sheol, behold, You are there.
> If I take the wings of the dawn,
> If I dwell in the remotest part of the sea,
> Even there Your hand will lead me,[122]

So God, if that is true," he continued as a prayer, while looking up into the sky, peering through the leaves on the trees, "You are with me now. There is no hiding from You. You've seen it all and know it all. You know my thoughts and my heart. You know I want to do better. I need to do better. Please, help me to do better."

As he continued walking he tried to pick apart the information about God and memorize it. It wasn't that he didn't have the passage memorized, but maybe it would help to be able to describe God without having to say the entire passage. By mid-morning he came up with a list that he could say and therefore see God's character in greater depth. His list began with: Searches me, knows my stance, understands me, knows me (who I am), knows every word before it is spoken, surrounds me, has vast knowledge, is present everywhere, and He will lead me.

Timothy continued walking and picking apart the passage for a good portion of the day. It was well into the afternoon when he finally began to see signs of another territory. He took a deep breath. He determined in his mind to make the best of it desperately not wanting to get caught there too. A quick glimpse at the first property showed that this land was not like that of Jacan. It was better kept, not spectacularly so, but much improved. He weighed his options. He could hurry through town and spend the night in the forest again, or he could rest here on the edge of the territory and then walk through early in the morning, or he could get a bite to eat then head out, or he could stay in someone's barn, or at their house for the night. The latter option was his last choice. He was afraid that what had happened at the last place might be a trap for him here at this place. He decided simply to walk through the territory and rest on the other side, hoping not to get "caught".

He walked through the town, a little briskly, but slow enough that it didn't appear as if he was in a hurry to get out. "Good evening sir! How would you like to rest yourself from your journey tonight? You look like you could use a nice comfortable place to stay. My family and I would be most grateful if you would spend the night at our place."

With so many travelers this time of year it was impossible for him to hide from view. Timothy hesitated. As much as he would love a rest, he wasn't so willing to trust that nothing would go wrong this time. Timothy looked over at the man, then glimpsed at his yard. Everything appeared to be okay. He did a double take when he saw a familiar figure in the background by a tree. It was Ross, he was nodding his head, as if to say, stay here for the night.

Timothy found himself nodding his head in return, more in response to Ross than to the man's question.

"Have you journeyed far?"

"Just over a week's worth of travel." He wasn't about to tell him that he had camped out for another week, distracted by his attempt to improve another man's property by his own power.

"Come on in, I was just heading in for the day. I was planning on doing some studying. It sure would be nice to have someone to bounce ideas off of, are you up for a discussion?

"Okay."

"I'm Jamshid,[123] pleased to have you come."

"Timothy. Thank you for having me."

The two headed inside after getting some feed for the lamb and making him a bed in what would be Timothy's room. Timothy was grateful; he did not want to spend any more time away from the lamb. He felt like he had neglected it too much already.

"So, you are headed to Jerusalem. My father left a couple of weeks ago. He loves it and always goes extra early and stays behind a few weeks. He says the conversations with others, the view of Christ, the resurrected saints, the rejoicing, and the whole atmosphere are just amazing. 'But be glad and rejoice forever in what I create; for behold, I create Jerusalem for rejoicing and her people for gladness.[124]' I guess that is where I get my love for discussion. I love to hear and learn from other people, just like my father. One day I would love to go to Jerusalem, but for now, I will learn as much as I can from others, people who are travelling. You know what I like best?"

"Uh, what is that?"

"I love it when people come and stay here on their way to Jerusalem and then pop back in on their way home to tell me what they've learned or what it was like. There is always such a change in people, especially first timers."

"I would imagine so. This is my first time going."

"Oh yeah?"

"Yeah, so I'm afraid if you want to talk about Jerusalem, the best I could do is tell you someone else's description, but as for myself, I'm not really sure what to expect so I don't have much to say."

"Yeah, that makes sense, you'd rather just wait to see what it is like then to hang on someone else's description. I get it. For me, all I get is someone else's description. And I am grateful for that. I love to set my imagination to work and let their experience come to life in my mind."

Timothy nodded his head, thankful he wouldn't have to discuss Jerusalem. He knew he wasn't ready. He was getting a little apprehensive though, as to where this conversation might lead.

"What is it that you do on your land?" Jamshid asked, as he sat in his kitchen chair. He pulled up to the table, offering Timothy a seat and a plate of food. Jamshid's wife also sat, they prayed then continued their conversation.

"I'm in charge of the garden. I love the plants, watching the life grow from a little seed into these extraordinary plants always amazes me." He paused for a moment, hesitated and then added, "God has blessed our territory."

"Ah yes, the plants. You can see so much of God in them, his nurturing nature. It reminds me of how we too are cared for by God and the resurrected saints, they desire to bring us closer to God, to our full potential as you desire the plants to reach their full maturity, potential and beauty. Do you feel as if you have reached your potential? What growth stage do you feel you are at?"

"My growth potential?" Timothy shook his head and rubbed his chin. He had never thought of his life being like a plant's. He had never thought that he was like that little seed, growing into what he was supposed to be.

"Yeah, you know, the reason God created you. Look at the resurrected saints for example. They lived their life, fulfilled their purpose and now they get to serve God in unity. They're amazing when they're together. I heard that in Jerusalem, when you see them together, although you can distinguish each one as separate, they all function as if they are one. They know what is going on and who needs what, like they can read each other's thoughts or something. They know just what the other one is doing and they fill in any part to make everything run so smoothly and flawlessly. It's just incredible. I can't describe it much better because I haven't seen it and the people I've heard it from just couldn't find the words to explain exactly what they meant."

"That's nice that they can all work together." Timothy's voice trailed off as he made the statement. His mind wasn't really on the resurrected saints, but on another question that he wanted to ask. He hesitated though, because he didn't want to be asked the same question in return. His desire to know was greater than the fear of coming up with his own explanation, not that he had ever tried to hide information from people before (other than his feelings or lack thereof about God to his family), so with a bit of hesitancy in his voice, he asked, "What do you feel is, uh, your purpose on earth?"

"Me, oh, well, actually I had a really hard time finding my purpose. There was what I thought I wanted and then there was what God had planned for me."

"What do you mean? What you thought your purpose was and what God planned it to be?"

"Well, my dream has always been to go to Jerusalem. For years I have been told of the wonders there. I was told that everything we have here is merely the blessings that come from our obedience and our going there. Here is only a little piece of what the entire picture is, here is only a reflection of the goodness we receive because of our obedience, but in Jerusalem, oh Jerusalem, what a sight that would be!" The man's face lit up and he had a faraway look in his eyes, as if he was imagining all the greatness of what he had ever been told about the city.

Timothy sat in stunned silence. Here was a man that should have been going to Jerusalem. The heart and passion in his voice and explanation were more pronounced than all of Timothy's most excited moments throughout his entire life. How could he possibly find this much passion between now and the 15th of Tishri? It didn't matter how hard he had tried to focus on that passage today, he didn't have an ounce of the emotion this guy did.

"But," he sighed, "like I said, my plan was not God's plan."

"What was or is God's plan for your life? Why couldn't you go to Jerusalem, surely that cannot be out of His will, even if you aren't the oldest child. I know some people who have travelled with the representative to see the great city."

"Oh, no. God has another plan for me and His plan is far greater than my plan. One day he may give me my greatest desire, but for now, my job is here, at home. I am to greet those who are travelling and give them a place to rest. I am to listen to their stories. I am to encourage those along the trail, those whose purpose it is to go and serve in Zion. You are the oldest, a representative, your purpose is to go and serve. You are to see our God in all His glory in His city, and to worship Him. You will see the resurrected saints working and coming from the New Jerusalem. You will be a part of the great sacrifice, the memory of the amazing past, the demonstration of God's great love to His people for all time. Me, I am to benefit from those travelers. I am to hear and learn from your stories. I am to share and encourage you with information from others along the same trail. Your journey is not easy. You are away from your family, you are in unfamiliar territory. You are to continue on, my job is to encourage, help and support you on your journey."

He spoke with such conviction and passion. There was no hesitancy in his voice. No question and no regret or upset feelings that he couldn't have what he wanted. Instead he loved his lot in life, he knew his purpose and he did it well. He brought glory to God right here and now because of his actions. If only Timothy could come to terms with his life, his purpose to serve, to go, to worship. His greatest desire was to garden, to prune, to grow. How could he learn to fulfill his purpose? How could his attitude change? "So how did you become okay with living for this purpose rather than the one you really desire?"

"Oh, it was not easy." He paused as he took a few bites of food and remembered his past. "It was a very long process. God had to show me that His plan was far better than mine, but before He could do that, I had to learn to trust Him. I had to be okay with never getting to see the city. Almost as if the idea and that part of my life had to die. I had to bury it. It was not until I was okay with the purpose that He gave me that I could mention or talk about the city without being jealous or upset. Until then I could not even begin to fulfill my purpose because the two overlapped so closely, yet they were different enough that it disturbed me for the longest time."

"What happened that changed your mind?" Timothy wondered. He hoped that he could gain some insight and perhaps it would be the key that would help change his attitude.

"Well, I was so miserable. My family had noticed. It had really gotten out of hand. I would always scowl at those who stayed here on their journey to Jerusalem. I would not help them at all. I really was terrible. Thankfully my wife stepped in. She told me that God would not honor the attitude I was displaying. One day she asked me, "Do you really think God would want you in the holy city with that attitude? He cannot bear to let such disgust near Him." It really caused me to think. Tearle[125], our resurrected saint, also had a few words to say. Actually, he really helped me to put all of my thoughts and reasons on paper. We then held a ceremony where I burned the list, giving my desires completely to God and told Him I would be willing to do whatever He had planned for my life."

"A ceremony, like giving up?"

"No, not giving up, more like giving over, allowing God to take the wheel and direction of my life."

Timothy chewed on that thought for a moment. It seemed to work for Jamshid, he was content to guide people and encourage people on their way to Jerusalem even though he was never promised to go there himself. They talked some more before Jamshid stated that he needed a good night's rest and it looked as if Timothy needed one too.

Timothy went to his room, still thinking about what he had heard, about what it would take for him to give up his dream.

"Here, I brought you some paper. I'm Tearle," The resurrected saint stated as he walked across the room. "Ross said you have some burdens to lie down, some desires that are not what God has planned for you. The best way to clearly identify those is to write them down, explain them all, exactly as you feel. Be honest, it is the only way to acknowledge your true feelings. There should be enough paper here. I'll come check on you later."

With that he was gone and Timothy found a stack of papers and a pen in his hand. Rest would not come now even though he felt emotionally drained, he had a task to complete. He felt desperate to express his needs, his feelings, without the worry of being looked down upon by his family for failing them. He had so much he wanted to say, so much he wanted others to understand about him, so much he felt he had kept secret for far too long. He sat down at the little desk in the room and began to write.

Chapter 16

"The absolute, honest truth, from Timothy," Timothy scrawled out first. "It's important that I say this and stick to it," he thought.

"It is a fact that should be well known to all, but not necessarily comprehended. I love gardening. In reality, I love everything that has to do with gardening. I love to watch plants grow. I love to cultivate and see the change in things. I love to see the fruit of my labor. I love the smell of the earth. I love the rain and the freshness of the dew. I love the early morning when the plants have their final growth stretch before the heat of the day. I love the peace and tranquility in the garden and orchard." His pen now seemed to write on its own, effortlessly he continued. "I love the fact that no one else is there. I love that I am in control and I nurture each plant so that it grows to its fullest potential. I have enough knowledge of plants to understand them and read them, to know what is best for them, whether it be more water or sun or nutrients in the soil. I love the bounty of the harvest after my work is done. My work is not in vain, for it is multiplied, like the loaves of bread in the story of Jesus or the parable about the minas. I get more than ten times the amount I plant. My harvests are always successful. I am able to provide excellent food for my family from the bounty of my crops. They enjoy and benefit from all the work I do. I have an important job, one that my family simply could not do without. I'm needed in the fields."

Timothy paused for a moment and read over the paragraph. Yes, that was definitely him and his love. That is how he felt. "I don't understand what is so wrong with this. Why should I have to give up something I love and Jamshid have to give up the idea of something he desperately wants. Why can't God just let anyone go from the family as a representative? Why does it have to be the oldest? Why can't I work in the garden? There is nothing wrong with it! Just because I'm firstborn, there's no law against it. I don't get it." Timothy ran his tense fingers through his hair, his frustration mounting.

"Tough question, but it can be answered."

Timothy spun around to see Tearle in the room. "I see you have a start on your list. That is excellent. What a great start. Do you see any problem with anything you wrote?"

Timothy looked puzzled as he reread the paragraph. Nothing jumped out to him.

"That little bit, right there," Tearle pointed to the paper, "I love that *I* am in control and *I* nurture each plant so that it grows to its fullest potential. Do you see a problem with that?"

Timothy's mind slowly turned, what could be wrong with that? Well, perhaps he didn't have full control, his father and grandfather still had some say in what he planted.

"Do you really think it is you that makes each plant grow? That it is solely your ability?"

Like a bolt of lightning the words of Amos' grandfather flashed into his mind, "It doesn't matter how great your ability, it was not laziness that caused this land to look like this and no matter how much effort you pour into this land, you will never get it to look like you want it to."

"So you are saying I have nothing to do with the growth of any plant? That all my work over the years has been for nothing and benefited my family nothing? What, do you think I just 'play' around the garden and pretend to grow things? Do you think I have no ability at all?"

"I didn't say you don't have ability. I merely pointed out that you are not in control of the garden. God is. Do not confuse His blessing with your ability. It is He who causes the plants to grow and to produce. It is He who blesses your land."

Oh how quickly Timothy had forgotten what he had learned at Amos'. He had so easily gotten caught up in the fields as he had done at home. It had been too easy for him to forget, too easy for the plants to consume him and for him to forget everything else. Although he was not physically stuck here, he was afraid that he might be stuck emotionally, forever attached to his love of the garden. He couldn't seem to help it. The possibility remained that he might never learn to love God as he should. He didn't think he could ever feel for God what he felt for his garden. He had never seen Him nor known Him. He couldn't see the works in his life, for goodness had always been there. How was he supposed to know that was just from God and not from the work of his ancestors or himself? What had he seen to show him that? Until Amos' farm he had never known anything but prosperous grounds.

"I'm wrong, Tearle. How, how do I change? I am consumed with gardening. It gives me purpose and fills my life."

"No, it does not. Your life is not full. You may think it is, but nothing can fill your life like God can. You have become satisfied with so little, but God wants so much more for you. You need to

> Turn your eyes upon Jesus,
> Look full in His wonderful face,
> And the things of earth will grow strangely dim,
> In the light of His glory and grace.[126]

Once you see His face - that will be all you need. You will then know what it is to fill up on Him. You must not let yourself be distracted.

Control your thoughts, be steadfast, think solely of Him, then you will know what love is and only then."

Again Tearle disappeared. He gave no further explanation and left no further instructions for Timothy. Timothy was left with a piece of paper that burned in his hand, a paper that he had poured out his heart on, only to be told that it was a pitiful substitute for what God wanted to fill him with, but he hadn't allowed it. How was he supposed to change unless someone told him how?

"Turn your eyes upon Jesus," he mumbled, "I can't see Him!"

He folded up the paper and shoved it in his bag, but not before he wrote down all the words that Tearle had recited. "Turn your eyes upon Jesus…and the things of earth with grow strangely dim…" If only he could make his love for the garden grow dim and his love for God increase, then this entire problem would be solved.

He lay down on the bed, the lamb assuming his place snuggled close beside him as he closed his eyes. He could see his beautiful gardens and orchards in his mind. They had grown and produced some of the best fruits and vegetables around. Many travelers that had passed through had commented on the beauty and flavor of *his* fruit. *His* fruit. As Timothy drifted off to sleep his orchards and gardens seemed to fade. A bright light was slowly overpowering them, blocking and hiding them from view. They paled in comparison to the bright light. It was so bright that Timothy could barely look into it. He would glance around the edges trying to gather some clue as to what the source of the light could be, but he couldn't figure it out. It soon took over the fields and every plant. He could see nothing left of his beloved garden, only this magnificent light. It dazzled his eyes and remained a steady brilliance while he slept.

When Timothy woke the light was gone. Only the sun from outside shone in, but the image remained in his mind as he readied for the day.

"Good morning Timothy, how did you sleep?"

"Well, thank you. I feel quite rested. I had the strangest dream though. I was thinking of my gardens and orchards back at home when this bright light began to appear in the midst of the fields. It continued to grow until there was nothing there but the light. It seemed to consume and over power everything."

"Hmmm, interesting. Perhaps God is trying to show Himself to you before you reach Jerusalem. He is the light.[127] His light will always overpower."

They continued to discuss God being the light that shines - the source of life and life itself. How He is the center, the true focus of the world.

Timothy thanked Jamshid for a place to stay and the food from supper and breakfast. He felt more confused than before, but he was still determined to continue on his journey. He wasn't sure how taking each step was an act of worship anymore than serving God by ministering to people passing by, or working in the garden, but since it was what he had been told to do, he knew it was obedience and that counted for more than anything right now.[128]

Chapter 17

On his way out of town he noticed another man who also seemed to be on a journey. Timothy quickened his pace to catch up to him. He thought company would be better than being left alone to his own thoughts and the confusing image from last night's dream.

"Good morning, I'm Timothy. I'm on my way to Jerusalem. Are you travelling there as well?" Timothy questioned.

"Peace be unto you.[129] I too am journeying to Jerusalem. It sure would be nice to have company. I'm Peter," the man held out his hand and delivered a firm handshake. "Nice little lamb you have there, for your sacrifice?"

"Yes, I was told to bring it."

"Oh. You don't sound too excited about that. Why didn't you just get one in Jerusalem?"

"My father told me to carry it with me. Something about the true meaning of sacrifice would come clear or be clearer if I carried a lamb. It has helped me to keep my muscles in shape as he's grown. I guess that could be considered one benefit. I haven't seen too many others yet."

Peter slowly shook his head, but made no further comment. They were silent for awhile as they walked through the forest. The forest with its lush green colors was filled with all kinds of vegetation and animals. At first Timothy didn't notice the animals, he still wasn't in tune to them as much as he was to plants, unless of course one was rustling a bush that he hadn't see before, but he was picking up on them a bit more. A few leaves shook on the bush nearest him and he saw the tail of a little lizard as it scurried down the branch. The lamb moved his head in acknowledgment and then nestled it closer to Timothy's body, settling in comfortably while Timothy walked.

"Is this your first time to represent your family?" Timothy asked, breaking the silence of the last few minutes.

"Oh no, I have gone many times before. It's my favorite time of the year. There is no greater love or desire that I have then to journey to Jerusalem and worship my LORD. 'Behold, this is our God for whom we have waited that He might save us. This is the LORD for whom we have waited; Let us rejoice and be glad in His salvation.'"[130]

Peter's face lit up with excitement as he continued to proclaim the greatness of the LORD. His hands were raised, extended to the heavens and his eyes were closed as he recited the blessing of the LORD. Timothy could feel a genuine love exuding from him for God and it bothered him that he might not be able to relate well to this man on the journey. His heart sank deeper. It seemed whomever he met was either way past his belief in God or didn't care about God at all. Was there no one on earth that questioned and kind of wondered just a little as he did? Anyone who wanted to believe, but struggled?

"When did you first realize that there was no greater thing than to serve our LORD?" Peter queried.

Timothy paused for a moment, in his thoughts and in his steps. He had always loved and served the LORD, he could not remember a time when he didn't, but he had never really felt it, at least not as fully as his father or grandparents had and apparently, not as much as Peter did either.

He adjusted the lamb and thought. He wasn't sure if he should share with him his doubting thoughts. It was more than a little strange and more than a little inappropriate for him not to have a complete love for the Lord. After all, he was going to Jerusalem. And even though the people from the past few days had been more than open with him, he wasn't sure he was completely ready to be totally honest. When he tried to pour out his heart, he had barely gotten started then Tearle showed up to point out how wrong he was. He figured it was probably best to veer on the side of caution and not express too much. "Uh, I have always served the LORD with my family."

"Yes, but when did you realize that there was no greater joy than serving the LORD?"

"No greater joy, I'm, uh, I'm not sure I understand." His serving had consumed him, in the garden, but apparently that had been the wrong serving. He was supposed to be serving as he journeyed to Jerusalem, but he sure felt anything but service walking this path the last couple of weeks.

Peter dove in to explain. "You see, everyone knows about the LORD,[131] they know to obey His commandments and follow His statutes, but that doesn't mean that it becomes a part of them, that it gives them life or knowledge of the LORD. We must listen to Him and learn how it is He wants us to serve and to live."

"Right, of course. What about yourself? When did you start serving?"

"Oh, I can remember it like it was yesterday." Peter started excitedly, "I had grown up in an amazing family. We all loved the Lord and sang His praises all the time, but the time when it became real to me was the first time my dad took me to Jerusalem. He told me, 'Son, I want you to travel with me. There are many things to see in this life, but there is only one thing worth living for. Although it will be many years before you will offer sacrifices for our family in Jerusalem, I know it is important for you to see this and not wait until you can go and offer sacrifices on your own. You need your love for God woven into everything you do. Our land has been well blessed. God has been good to us. I want you to see firsthand just how amazing He really is. I don't want you to take what we have for granted. I want you to know.' And know I did. I was so young to be going, only 21, but nothing has ever impacted me as much as that. To see the sights and sounds, to feel the anticipation for the lead up of seeing Him, it was incredible! There were hundreds of thousands of people milling about lambs, oxen, and doves were everywhere. It was an incredible sight, but the best part was seeing Him. That was indescribable! I knew from that moment on that I would never doubt what God had done for me. His love was clearer than ever and I've pledged my whole life to His service." Peter's eyes were glowing and an extra bounce was in his step as he gained momentum and excitement from what he shared.

"Wow, that intrigues me. I can't wait to get there."

Peter couldn't stop now, he was on a roll. "It is nothing like you could ever imagine. God is there in all His glory. It is His perfect love enacted that makes it so wonderful. You can see it and feel it even before you enter the city, but once you see His face, there is nothing on this earth that can compare. Everything fades and seems dim next to Him. And the resurrected saints, you should see them when they get together! Why, I've always enjoyed seeing our resurrected saint and talking to him, but when you see him together with the others, it's incredible. You've never seen anything so unified. They all work together, as one. They each have their defined roles, but the way they work together unifies[132] their entire effort, so it seems that they effortlessly complete these amazing tasks and help all kinds of people. Their actions compliment and fill in for each other as one unified source. And they do this all while singing praises to the King. It's just absolutely incredible!"

"That sounds amazing. I can't imagine. I know Ross, our resurrected saint, has told me many stories about some other resurrected saints, even some of their lives before, when they lived on earth, but I can't imagine him with many others working together. I guess I've always seen him alone."

"Yes, but you know what? Wherever you see them, aren't they always working and serving Him? They are never rushed, but their goal is simply to keep us pointed in His direction."

"Yes, I guess so."

"They have their purpose, they know what to do. They don't question or wonder, they know that serving God is the only thing worthwhile. They go from place to place talking to or helping out or guiding anyone who has need. They are so genuine!"

"They are something, aren't they? Hey, hold up a minute, I need to put this lamb down and let him graze for a bit. He may not need as much food because he isn't exerting a lot of energy, but he does still need to eat and walk some."

"Yeah, sure. We could take a break. How do you like taking care of him?"

"It took a while to get used to, but it's not so bad, I guess. It definitely didn't come naturally that's for sure. It's not my calling, but he kind of just follows me around and eats and sleeps so that makes it easy."

"Yeah, I guess. Some may think of it as a burden that can cause problems. There are so many things that you must watch for, in order for it not to get hurt, for it to have no spot or blemish in order to be accepted as a sacrifice in the temple. Sometimes you may think that you'll be glad to be rid of it, but when the times comes to give up this little lamb, it won't be so easy. This little guy is so sweet and calm and hasn't done anything to cause anyone harm or real trouble and yet it must die. Suddenly, it won't seem so fair, it won't seem right. The lamb also won't seem like so much trouble or like a burden as you may have felt. The justice that everyone talks about and you see in society today seems to momentarily disappear. It is because death here is practically unheard of. It is so rare for a person to die even at 100. They are so young, but seeing this young lamb of one, die for you, for your family, whether you like taking care of the lamb or not, well, it just doesn't seem quite right at first.

"Only afterwards does the picture come into focus, 'Behold the Lamb of God which takes away the sin of the world.[133]' We are too young to have seen the evil of this world before the LORD came to rule, we know only what we have been told by our great ancestors about the evil, selfishness, cruelty and hate of this world. To think that Jesus was beaten, shamed, spit upon, and hanged on a cross[134] is more than I can imagine. I only know Him as the glorious king sitting on His throne in such majesty.

"But then, you'll watch this little, innocent lamb die, and you'll begin to see the cruelty and realize that your own heart was not perfect. It wasn't good enough. This little lamb had to die for you to have contact with God. Days go by, you'll see hundreds of sacrifices, and as you are in Jerusalem and sitting in your sukkot[135] you'll begin to really think about what it all really means – what He really did for you and what your response of worship and service to God means to you. Then there will be the rejoicing, the waving of branches as many rejoice,[136] can you really fake that? Oh to see His glory. You will never be the same again. You can't possibly be so nonchalant about it once you've seen it. Once you truly understand, you'll change, you'll see."

They came to a clearing in the forest as the sun lowered and cast a yellow, orange glow. They decided to rest for the night. Their conversation stayed animated all evening, with Peter doing most of the talking, as they ate, cared for the lamb and prepared for bed. Even after they had spread their blankets on the earth and the sky became dark Peter talked.

Slowly the talking dimmed and the two, with the lamb ever near Timothy, finally lay in the semi quite, listening to the sounds of the forest. Monkeys chattered their last goodnights, birds bid their farewell and Peter began a soft snoring. The conversation of the day ran through Timothy's mind. Peter sure had enough energy when describing the city. His eyes glowed, his steps lightened and he simply bounced as he talked. It must be absolutely spectacular.

With a heavy sigh Timothy wondered if he would or could ever get to the point of talking about the city with the same excitement, or even half the excitement. He was determined to go. He had promised himself and his family that much, but he sure hoped the feelings would follow. The ones everyone seemed to have, the great love and appreciation, were all the ones that he seemed to lack. He absently stroked the lamb as it lay peacefully beside him. The lamb seemed not to have a care in the world. He just followed and obediently journeyed with Timothy.

They woke early in the next morning. The lamb was up first, stretching and getting up to nibble on some nearby plants and drink from the stream. The men ate some berries from a bush nearby and some food that was given to them from the last homes they had visited. Timothy remained somewhat quiet as he was still trying to process all the excitement that

Peter had shown. He wondered if today would be similar. He also tossed the thought of his purpose back and forth and how he could possibly cause his love of the garden to lessen and his love for God to increase.

Peter seemed to pick up on Timothy's silence. He began softly, "You know, the way I figure it, is that we "were made by God and for God and until [we] understand that - life will never make sense[137]" to us."

Timothy stared at Peter for a moment. 'Were his thoughts so obvious to Peter? Was he really that easy to read?' "So, what if we don't understand our purpose? You see, in the last territory I stayed with a fellow who knew what his purpose was, although he said it was not the same as his greatest desire or at least what his greatest desire used to be. So how can you know your purpose if it's not the thing you want to do most in life? If it's not the passion that flows through your veins? Didn't God design us with a bent, something we are better at, a gift that we can use to serve Him? Wouldn't that gift and passion and service all be the goal of our life that is directed in service to God?"

"I guess they could be, although not necessarily. Sometimes God has more for us than we think at first or has been revealed to us. I think He wants us to search Him out, to learn more about Himself and ourselves. Unfortunately we are satisfied with the simple things that we already have and aren't willing to see if there is more for us. I guess that's why I want to serve God with my full heart. Keep growing, keep searching, keep finding if there is another way or thing He has for me to do so that I can serve and worship Him better."

"But isn't there something to be said for being content? Shouldn't you "be content with what you have?[138]" Shouldn't you just be satisfied with what He originally gave you?"

"Yes, it is important to be content. However, I think being satisfied in your relationship with God is not healthy. We should never sit back and think that we are close enough or know enough about God that we don't need to learn more or try and become more like Him. Just think, in the New Jerusalem, which is where the resurrected saints live, God is there. Yet, they are constantly working and serving and teaching others more about God. They never stop. They want to serve more. God is so infinite how could anyone understand every facet there is to know about Him? That is one of the things that makes Him so great and so amazing. There is no end to who He is. 'Oh, the depth of the riches both of the wisdom and knowledge of God! How unsearchable are His judgments and unfathomable His ways!'[139]"

Timothy felt a bit overwhelmed and definitely lost. He didn't really know God that well. Perhaps that was why he could not feel the same as the others. How could he worship or get excited about something he didn't know much about. His plants he knew well, he could be excited about them from any aspect – from planting to harvesting to storing and eating, because he knew so much about them. But about God, He had to admit, his knowledge was limited. He couldn't offer the praise that his father, grandfather and great grandfather gave because he had never taken the time to memorize praise passages as they had. The ones that they had studied together or he had been taught as a little boy, he could somewhat remember, but not well, because he had never really been interested. Perhaps if he had tried harder or listened better he would know more, but the truth was he hadn't, and now since he had come to find himself with this responsibility of offering a sacrifice in Jerusalem for his family, he was, for the first time in his life, wishing he would have spent a little more time listening to his elders. But he hadn't, and now he would pay for it by being and feeling very unprepared.

"Why don't you meditate on some Scriptures? That should help to show you the way. It says in the book of Psalms "Thy word is a lamp unto my feet and a light unto my path.[140]"

"Do you recommend any? I'm afraid I'm a bit rusty in that department. I was thinking of Psalm 139 earlier, but I'm afraid that was the best I could do."

"Oh, that is an excellent psalm too.
You scrutinize my path and my lying down,
And are intimately acquainted with all my ways.
Even before there is a word on my tongue,
Behold, O Lord, You know it all.

> You have enclosed me behind and before,
> And laid Your hand upon me.
> *Such* knowledge is too wonderful for me;

"Too wonderful, to…" he paused, looking heavenward and praising God, "He already knows everything. He is so great!

> I can do no hiding from Him.[141]

"What an incredible psalm and so comforting too. I love the fact that God knows everything about me. He has covered my physical body and my internal thoughts, He knows it all. It just amazes me at how great our God is. How about the hundredth Psalm for another one? It is short and easy and full of information."

"Okay."

They spent the rest of the day, working together memorizing and discussing Psalm 100.

> Shout joyfully to the LORD, all the earth.
> Serve the LORD with gladness;
> Come before Him with joyful singing.
> Know that the LORD Himself is God;
> It is He who has made us, and not we ourselves;
> *We are* His people and the sheep of His pasture.
> Know that the LORD Himself is God;
> It is He who has made us, and not we ourselves;
> *We are* His people and the sheep of His pasture.
> Enter His gates with thanksgiving
> *And* His courts with praise.
> Give thanks to Him, bless His name.
> For the LORD is good;
> His lovingkindness is everlasting
> And His faithfulness to all generations.

Thankfully Peter spent the majority of the time talking[142] about verse three. Knowing more about God who made them and how He wants responsibility for them and yet He wants to give them responsibility too. He was grateful that they didn't dwell on entering with thanksgiving and praise into the gates because he knew he wasn't ready for that yet. He wondered if it would be okay just to pretend, shouting and praising on his way into the city with the others, even if he didn't really mean it or feel it. But from their discussions he knew that God would know his heart, there was no fooling Him. For now, he would learn to focus on God's goodness and the fact that He was in control.

Chapter 18

The next day was another Sabbath. Timothy could hardly believe that he had left his home about three weeks ago. He had met some people whom he would consider friends and hoped that they would stay in touch. He was grateful for the input they had in his life. He knew it was important. In some ways he felt as if they had just as much if not more influence on him than his father had throughout his life. Somehow seeing other people and hearing their perspective made things seem more realistic to him.

When Timothy sat up he noticed a piece of paper sticking out of the corner of his bag. He reached for it and opened it up. In what he assumed was Peter's writing was another Psalm. He proceeded to read it.

May there be abundance of grain in the earth on top of the mountains;
Its fruit will wave like the cedars of Lebanon;
And may *those from the city flourish* like vegetation of the earth.
May <u>his name endure forever</u>;

> May his <u>name increase</u> as long as the sun shines;
> And let men bless themselves by him;
> Let all nations call him blessed.
> Blessed be the Lord God, the God of Israel,
> Who <u>alone works wonders</u>.
> And blessed be <u>His glorious name forever</u>;
> And may the whole earth be filled with His glory.
>
> Psalm 72:16-19

Timothy looked around after he finished reading it. Peter was nowhere in sight. His belongings were gone too. Had he left Timothy here to finish the journey alone? Who could blame him? He probably didn't want to make the rest of his favorite journey with a man who couldn't praise God and wasn't even excited about going to Jerusalem. What a disappointment he was. Timothy wished he would have at least said good-bye before taking off in the middle of the night, but then again, he guessed he understood. He hoped he wouldn't bump into him once they were in Jerusalem; that might be awkward.

Since Timothy didn't plan to travel on the Sabbath he didn't pack up his things. Instead he found a nearby stream and washed up and ate some breakfast. The little lamb was content munching on the fresh grass in the shade of the forest. Timothy sat back down on his blanket and reread the psalm that Peter had left.

He noticed that pieces of the psalm were underlined. Those pieces told of God. Timothy decided to memorize them and meditate on the new facts that he could learn from this passage.

"May his name endure forever." That would be a whole lot longer than his great grandfather was old. Imagine to be known across time, generation after generation. Years after people are gone and forgotten, He will still be remembered. But, not just be remembered, may his name increase, becoming greater and better known. I can't imagine! His name is already everywhere. His name is on the lips of everyone." He then thought of Amos, "Well, nearly everyone."

Timothy couldn't think of one other person who could be so well talked about. No one was famous or well known more than the LORD. He tried to remember back to stories his great-grandfather told him about the world ruler before Christ came to rule. He was a man to be feared, well, he wasn't really a man, he was so evil; he was the anti-Christ. He had done terrible things to believers. He had been well known, but thankfully his time had come to an end.

He tried to remember anyone else that may have been well known. When he was little he used to ask Ross a lot of questions from the past. What life had been like, what people did… Ross was very scant in his descriptions. He had said, "The world, as it was when I lived on it, was very unlike this one. Most people did not recognize God as king and would not acknowledge Him in any way. Their lives were poor and unsatisfying. They did not live with the purpose God intended." He would never go into more detail than that, saying that he would much prefer to talk about God and what He had done, for He was the reason for living and the one who gave us our purpose in life. Timothy remembered he had always felt somewhat disappointed, like there was a world out there that he was missing, a world that he wished he could have been a part of, even if only for a short time.

He looked down at the next line, "Who alone works wonders. Hmmm," he thought, "Who alone works wonders. Meaning, no one else does anything that is wonderful." His thoughts started to whirl and he began to wonder how that could possibly be true. "I mean, look at this earth, from what I see it is all wonderful. My garden is wonderful. You can't say I didn't have a part in it. To just leave it, would have meant ruin for it. Well, *I* think it would have. I know Tearle didn't agree, but you can't say that I didn't have a little something to do with it."

The phrase stuck in his head though. "Who ALONE works wonders." God did not need Timothy. God chose Timothy and let Timothy serve for His purpose, so that He could love him, but He was perfectly capable of surviving without him.

Timothy paused for a moment and looked around. The trees towered over him, the stream rippled past and his little lamb lay resting in the ankle high grass. The forest was beautiful. He had enjoyed examining each new tree and bush. He loved looking at the plants, the colors of the flowers, the variety. It was all amazing to him. It struck him for the first time; there was no one who cared for the jungle. The animals weren't "caretakers" of it. They just lived in it and benefited from its bounty. If the forest could look this amazing with little to no assistance, other than God, maybe he had not had such a great effect on his property after all. "He alone works wonders. He does not need me, but He still wants me."

The thought continued to grow in his mind throughout the day. It was hard to change his way of thinking and see things from a different perspective, but perhaps it held some validity. It wasn't until mid-afternoon that he looked at and thought of the last underlined phrase in the psalm. "Blessed be His glorious name forever."

"If he alone works wonders, then only His name can be blessed." Timothy thought. "If only His name is blessed, then only His name can increase and last forever, because it is all His doing. If it is all His doing, then the works I do are simply works of His wonder, not mine. I am a work of His wonder. My gardens are a work of His wonder. I don't work my own wonders."

The thought caused Timothy to pause, as if in a frozen stupor. Nothing he had done had been by his own doing or for his own praise. It wasn't that he had been praised by anyone that made him feel great, only his own self. It was his pride that thought he had accomplished all the work that he had done. He realized now that no one had ever told him before what a great job he was doing, the reason was probably because they realized it wasn't his work. How incredibly insensitive and selfish he had been to think that he could be in charge of something. That his works were comparable or better noted than God's. It was an embarrassing and humbling moment for Timothy.

He sat up for a good portion of the night, asking for forgiveness and for God to give him a change of heart. He had been so selfish. How great was God's wonder compared to what he thought he had accomplished. The realization that none of what he had done had been his doing more than bothered him. He felt guilty and unworthy to face this journey knowing what he had done and how he had thought. Could he really face the

King? Could he offer this sacrifice in thanksgiving and praise feeling such humility? Little did he know that the wonder he now understood was no comparison to what he would see one day soon.

The thoughts just made him sick inside as he tried to rest. He finally fell into a fitful sleep in the early morning hours; the lamb next to him seemed to be more of a disturbance then a comfort. He was awakened when he felt a tap on his shoulder.

"Are you ready to head out? We have land to cover today."

"Peter?" Timothy woke with the question on his lips. "I thought you had travelled on."

"No, I thought you could use some time to think, alone. I wasn't too far. How was your day?"

Timothy explained to him what he had learned from the psalm he had left. "I feel so humiliated. I can't believe that I would think I was capable of anything. How selfish and conceited I am."

"We all are. We must be so thankful that God is a forgiving God. He loves us. His love is great and extends far beyond our worst thoughts and deeds. Here's another passage from the Scriptures. I thought we could meditate on this today as we travel. There is nothing more important than 'listening to God's Word and receiving it as the Holy Spirit interprets it, in application to' ourselves.[143]"

Peter handed him another piece of paper. Timothy read the words carefully.

"Then you will say on that day,
I will give thanks to You, O LORD;
For although You were angry with me,
Your anger is turned away,
And You comfort me.
Behold, God is my salvation,
I will trust and not be afraid;
For the LORD GOD is my strength and song,
And He has become my salvation.
Therefore *you will joyously draw water*

> From the springs of salvation.
> And in that day you will say,
> 'Give thanks to the LORD, call on His name.
> *Make known His deeds* among the peoples;
> *Make them remember that His name is exalted.*'
> Praise the LORD in song, for He has done excellent things;
> *Let this be known throughout the earth.*
> Cry aloud and shout for joy, O inhabitant of Zion,
> For great in your midst is the Holy One of Israel."[144]

Timothy noticed again that parts about God were underlined. He also noticed that parts that referred to him were in a different kind of writing.

"Thank you. It is amazing that you gave me this today when I need to hear of God's forgiveness. He will not be angry forever. I knew that, but I didn't. I never had reason to think that God was angry with me before. I know better now and I'm grateful that He is a forgiving God."

"He is. Not only should we be grateful, but because of His character and His response to us we are then able to respond as we should to Him. When he forgives us and His anger is not against us, then we can be grateful. It is then that our praise can come forth. Our praise is released and sent up to God. We don't have to plan it out or pretend it, it just comes, it overflows like a spring, as it should from our grateful heart."

"Yes, you're right. Hey, did you notice this kind of overlaps with Psalm 72?"

"How so?"

"About making His name known. In Psalm 72 it said that His name would endure forever and would increase."

"And so it will. As we are forgiven and realize His greatness we are the ones to spread it and help it increase. We are His works of wonder that He uses to spread His praise."

They walked for a while each in their own thoughts. Peter, praising God for Timothy coming to a realization of His greatness as well as just praising God for all He does. Timothy thinking how amazing it was that God would still want his sacrifice, even when he thought he had been the one to have such great accomplishments and when he had no desire to go to Jerusalem at all. He was grateful that God was so forgiving.

The men continued walking together and sharing God's Word as the days passed. They travelled through many towns, staying with various people and they slept many nights in the forest or grasslands. Sometimes their conversation was full and vibrant, other times it was quiet and reflective, but it was always about God.

Chapter 19

After many days they arrived at the port city on the river. Together they were to purchase or obtain supplies, catch a boat, and continue the next leg of the journey heading northwest up the river.

The ship they took was not large. It was powered by great sails. Because of the Feast of Booths soon approaching, the ship was more crowded than usual. Various people from all over the continent were settling in, some had traveled this route[145] many times before; others were novices, like Timothy. Peter and Timothy settled their few belongings and food by their bunks and headed up on the deck for some sea breeze. Timothy carried the lamb with him.

They reached the bow and paused by an older man, he looked like he was in his late 300s. He turned in greeting towards them, "Come, let us go up to the mountain of the LORD, to the house of the God of Jacob; that He may teach us concerning His ways and that we may walk in His paths."[146]

"Let us go at once to entreat the favor of the LORD, and to seek the LORD of hosts; I will also go,"[147] responded an elated Peter.

"There is no greater time of the year, then when I get to go to Jerusalem and see the wisdom, understanding, counsel, strength, knowledge,[148] loving-kindness, faithfulness, justice and righteousness of the LORD.[149] Oh praise His name, 'Give thanks to the LORD, call on His name, Make known His deeds among the peoples; make them remember that His name is exalted.'[150] Are we not blessed to be on such a journey?" Peter immediately shook his hand and continued to praise the LORD with him. Timothy was still a bit hesitant, he glanced at his lamb, forever by his side, then back at the man who was radiating praise and glory to the LORD. It was clear from the expression on his face alone that he had a heart full of praise, dedicated to God.

Timothy stood and listened to Peter and Meyer[151] Abdiel,[152] as the older man had introduced himself. They each proclaimed the LORD's goodness. All of this was familiar to him, he had heard his father, grandfather, even great grandfather speak of many of the same things. They all had this extra zeal, this extra glow, this extra vibrant love for the LORD that seemed to be lacking in him. He was learning. He had learned much from Peter on their journey so far. Peter had taught him many scriptures. He not only memorized them, but they also discussed every aspect of them, picking them apart so that Timothy could really see who God was and is and how much praise was required from him. But it still didn't flow naturally from him as it did from Peter, Meyer and his family.

Chapter 20

The boat ride was to take a little more than a week. In spite of Timothy's anxiety about reaching the city, he was looking forward to seeing the land. He had heard from numerous people on the boat that the land from the sea to the city was simply magnificent. There was nothing on earth that could compare with the lushness of the foliage or the exuberance of the people. Apparently the colors were so vibrant and beautiful that it left many a man at a loss for words. The place simply couldn't be described as it deserved to be.

Timothy's ears always perked up when he heard someone describing the landscape. He listened intently to see what he might learn of the land or new plant life. Although he did not want it to consume him, his ears still had a natural tendency to catch such information.

One night, as he lay on his bunk, the lamb nestled near the foot of the bed, he tried to imagine what the grounds might look like. He tried to picture his home, even more vibrant with extensive types of plants, but he was never satisfied. He never felt he could imagine it correctly.

As he lay there feeling the gentle rocking of the boat he heard someone clearing their throat. He had a feeling that it was meant to get his attention, so he slowly opened his eyes, half hoping no one would be there to disturb his imaginative thoughts. But there was someone.

Ross was sitting across from his bed, just looking at him, knowingly, as if disappointed in him for not doing a better job at controlling his thoughts. Timothy felt ashamed. He knew that he was supposed to be meditating on God and who He is, but somehow, as always, the plants took precedence.

"What has Peter taught you these past days and weeks?"

"Uh, Scriptures."

"Yes, about what? About plants?"

"No."

"Why is it that you are so taken with plants, when your mind should be training to think only of God? Plants will not survive forever, nor can they give you anything. You need to control your mind, to take every thought captive. You can't simply let it wander to the pleasures that you desire. You must train it to focus on Him and Him alone. Nothing else should creep into your thoughts. You should allow nothing else to stay there!"

"I know, it's just."

"No, you don't know. There can be no excuses. It is what you need to do. Final. End of discussion, end of trying to persuade yourself it's not so bad. [You] 'are taking every thought captive to the obedience of Christ,[153]' not to the obedience of yourself or to your own pleasures either. Everything against Him must be destroyed, put away. It's time for you to be in control of your mind, stop letting it be lazy and wander around. Take charge!"

With that Ross was gone. He didn't leave time for any more argument, he just said what he came to say and left.

"Ugh. And here I thought he was supposed to guide me, not fuss me out then leave me to my own devices!" Timothy put his head back on his pillow. He shook his head in frustration and closed his eyes.

Then Timothy felt something slip into his hand. He lifted it toward his head and once again peered through the slits in his eyes. He was about to make another comment, but when he fully opened his eyes, he noticed that no one was there.

He looked at the piece of paper again and opened it. The writing was familiar to him. It was Ross'. He had left a verse. "I guess this is my guidance. Thanks." He let out a sigh, then leaned toward the window to catch the moonlight and read the verse aloud.

"You will keep him in perfect peace, whose mind is stayed on You, because he trusts in You."[154]

"So that was why Ross was so adamant," Timothy thought. "He knew that my mind was in turmoil and that I was easily led away from God. But he also knew God's promise. If only I could fully trust Him and Ross and others. I just don't see how to let go, to 'control' my mind. It is naturally filled with what I know and love, my garden."

Hold every thought captive. Mind at perfect peace. Take every thought captive. Mind at perfect peace. Mind stayed on Him. Perfect peace. Mind stayed on Him. Perfect peace.

The words swam round and round in his head as he lay in his bunk. If only he could. Was it possible? What difference would it make? Was it too late, he was 85? Could he really retrain his brain?

He wasn't lazy. He could control his mind. If that is what it took, then Timothy could do it. He'd focus on these new scriptures and some other scriptures, unfortunately, he felt like he was wearing those Scriptures out. He hadn't gotten any new thoughts from them other than the thoughts that he and Peter had discussed. Perhaps he should try looking at them from another angle, but he wasn't sure how. Somehow, he figured, this was going to be a long night.

Chapter 21

Early the next morning Timothy awoke from his brief night's rest. "Focus," was his goal for the day. He decided to take his lamb on the deck and feed him there while he waited for the sun to rise and the others to get up from their night's sleep. His thoughts were still on last night's scolding from Ross. Mind control, it felt like a game. Which thoughts could remain in your mind the longest and remain the most coherent? Should your attitude and likes have something to do with it? Or was it pure selfishness to simply let your mind think about the things you wished to think on? Timothy wasn't sure, he decided to rummage through his mental files and find a scripture that might help him focus more on God.

He reached the bow of the boat and was surprised to see Meyer kneeling in front of one of the benches. He had been quite impressed with Meyer over the last few days. Of all the people he had ever met, this man had a heart for God that surpassed them all. Not only did he constantly talk about the LORD, but everything he said seemed to have relevance and place. It seemed to help make each conversation closer and more purposeful, more than he had ever heard before.

Meyer heard the steps as Timothy and the lamb approached him. At first he stayed focused on his prayer, giving his fullest attention to that, but then he felt that it would be best for him to use this time to speak with Timothy. Although he had seen Timothy on a number of occasions since they met on the ship he had not yet had time to have a one on one talk with him. He was interested in talking to Timothy and wanted hear his thoughts. What did he really think and feel about this journey? Why was he going? He sure didn't seem excited like everyone else on the boat. He didn't join in with his own praises; he merely watched and listened to everyone else as they gave their praises.

Timothy was about to walk quietly to the stern of the boat when Meyer motioned for Timothy to join him. Meyer stood, turned and then sat on the bench he had just been kneeling at. There was silence for a moment, Timothy allowing Meyer to begin the conversation as the elder of the two, as well as not being really sure what he should say. This man always spoke of God, in such a loving and caring fashion, what Timothy would say could not compare and he didn't want to sound ignorant or disheartening. Timothy's eyes shifted to and fro, from the lamb to the floor to the side of the boat. They didn't lift very far and most certainly did not look into Meyer's face. He put some of the grass he had carried on the deck for the lamb to munch on while they sat.

"What are you afraid of?"

Timothy jumped slightly as he was taken aback. This man whom he had only ever heard sing or speak praises to God was asking a question about him. Not proclaiming God to him. He felt uncovered, as if Meyer could see right through him, to his very soul. What had he seen, how had he read his thoughts? What would cause him to focus on something like this other than God? Timothy didn't think he noticed little things in life. He figured all he was concerned about was praising God.

Timothy gave him a puzzling expression at first, hoping to hide his surprise. At the same instant he realized that he could hide nothing from this man. This man who seemed so close to God, who exuded His character, had asked him a question, point blank. There was no demise or accusations, only a desire to know the truth. Timothy hung his head in shame. "I'm not good enough. I can't offer the sacrifice worthily. I am going to fail my family."

"Yes, yes. You are right. You are not good enough, neither am I, nor anyone else for that matter."

"Yes you are. You sing His praises all of the time. Your face glows whenever you speak of Him. You bring Him glory, honor and joy. This is your calling, your purpose, you have mastered what you are supposed to do. Me, I'm so inadequate. I can't even sing half a song well, let alone feel like I truly mean it. I can only recite a few Scriptures and most of them I don't get the meaning of and I sure can't tell you which ones to say at which occasion. I can't tell you which ones are about God or myself or anyone else! Worst of all, I don't know what my purpose is, because what I'm good at God doesn't want me to do, but what I can't do, God expects me to. It's too hard. I can't focus or remain dedicated to this cause. I'm a failure! Why can't I just stay home in my garden?"

"It is all part of the journey." Meyer began slowly, nodding his head, like an elderly grandfather in complete agreement. "The realization of how unworthy we really are. How none of us can accomplish anything. It is all done through His good work. He works through us, using us, just because He can, not because we can. We are to do what we can for Him, not in our way, but in His. Let go and let Him lead. Once you realize this is your purpose you will realize that life comes together, it fits, like a puzzle, like you with God. It just works."

"But I don't even know Scriptures. I don't know which ones to say in greetings to people or which ones to go into the city with, or approach the temple, or see God, or go home and explain what has happened, or share with someone who…"

"Well, now, that's an easy fix." Meyer turned slightly and picked up a book that was beside him. The sparkle in his eyes told Timothy that this book was special to him. "Here," he continued, "study this. It has all of your answers and more, even answers to questions you haven't asked. Become familiar with this book. The more you know it and use it the more it will guide you and the more you will know God which will then tell you how you are to fulfill your purpose."

Timothy carefully reached over and took the book. He turned it over in his hands. He had never held one before, but he knew this had to be the book that contained the history of the world. This was the book with the stories of God, the Scriptures that would tell him more.

"Looking at it from the outside isn't going to help you. It's what's on the inside that counts. Why don't you sit on this bench? I need to walk around. I'll bring some food for your lamb. You take your time and find something out about God. 'Taste and see that the Lord *is* good; blessed *is* the man *who* trusts in Him!'[155] It's time you went on your own discovery adventure rather than just letting others feed you."

Chapter 22

Timothy slowly opened the book. He wasn't sure where to look first. There were so many pages, so many chapters, so many verses, so much he didn't know, and so many places to look. How would he know which was the right place to start?

So he flipped. The first place he paused was at Deuteronomy 3. There was a verse that was circled, it said, "O Lord GOD, You have begun to show Your servant Your greatness and Your strong hand; for what god is there in heaven or on earth who can do such works and mighty acts as Yours?"[156]

"Okay," thought Timothy, "show me Your mighty works and acts that you do. Help me to know You God." He remembered the list he had written down in Amos' book. God had shown him plenty in the past and in the present. He had not remembered to continually watch for God's goodness. His mind had been focused on things that were important to him, not God.

Timothy flipped again, coming to a prayer in I Kings 8:23. "O Lord, the god of Israel, there is no God like You in heaven above or on earth beneath, keeping covenant and showing lovingkindness to Your servants who walk before You with all their heart."

"Walk before You," Timothy reread, "with all their heart. Walk, worship in action, with all my heart. What is my heart? My desire? My what? What is that supposed to look like?" Timothy put the Bible beside him for a moment and for the first time this morning looked out over the sea. The sun was just beginning to rise over the horizon. The glow cascaded a brilliant red and orange across the sky in a v formation. The water was dark, only showing the reflection from the sun at the center, in front of the glow. The silhouette of the trees on the banks and whatever may have been hiding amongst them did not capture Timothy's attention like the colors of the sky.

"My heart, my center. To follow with my heart is to shine from within, letting the things dearest to my heart shine forth. What is on the outskirts, the fringes, merely fades away in the shadows. What was it grandfather used to say? He said it was the old Jewish Shema. It had something about heart." Timothy flipped through the Bible again, trying to remember what the reference was. After some time he came to it back in Deuteronomy.

"Hear, O Israel! The LORD is our God, the LORD is one! You shall love the LORD your God with all your heart and with all your soul and with all your might. These words, which I am commanding you today, shall be on your heart.[157] That's it!" Timothy shouted. He jumped from the bench and repeated the words that lit the beginning ember of his heart, "'The LORD is one!' There is no other. None can replace. He is like the sun, the one that shines on us, the brilliant over powering light. Without His full light I am but the silhouette of the trees on the bank at dawn. I am nothing. I look like nothing and can do nothing, but when His light shines on me and in me and through me, and I am in the center of His will, His work can be accomplished. It is that which causes everyone to sing praises. He is the LORD!"

Timothy could barely contain his excitement as he watched the sun continue to rise. Everything started to come alive. Before everything had been hidden, overshadowed, dark. You could not see its purpose or even what it was. It was not until the light shone on them that you could see the item and its importance. Nothing could be identified or had any beauty without that light. God is that light. That light in people was what caused them to be beautiful and to shine.

The sky was full of colors now. The reds had turned to purples with a pale blue sky above. Timothy felt like the very heavens had opened and he could rise into the sky. His smile stretched across his face, the light from without and within shining on him, in him and through him.

"I get it! I get it!" Timothy grabbed the lamb and spun around. You are important because of the Son. I am important because of the Son. It is His light that will tell us what to do. Timothy leaped with excitement toward Meyer, who was approaching with the food. Still holding the lamb, with a brilliant smile stretched across his face, he tried to explain to Meyer what had happened. His words jumbled up a bit, but he was able to express what was in his heart. It was the LORD, His light that was shining.

Meyer grabbed him by the arm. "I am so pleased. God knew you would understand. He would not have you come to His city without realizing this great importance. You're journey has just begun. Now you can really understand what is going on and join in the praise. Come, let us find a psalm to sing in praise to His name because of your revelation." The food and the lamb were set down as together they looked in the Word of God to find a Scripture to memorize for this joyous occasion.

"Ah, here we go." Meyer stated,

> "O come, let us sing for joy to the LORD,
> Let us shout joyfully to the rock of our salvation.
> Let us come before His presence with thanksgiving,
> Let us shout joyfully to Him with psalms.
> For the LORD is a great God
> And a great King above all gods,
> In whose hand are the depths of the earth,
> The peaks of the mountains are His also.
> The sea is His, for it was He who made it,

And His hands formed the dry land."[158]

"That's perfect," Timothy stated, joining him in the praise song. Together they memorized, recited, sang and meditated on the words. People were just starting to come up from below deck. Some with a little sleep still in their eyes, but when they saw Timothy and Meyer praising God on the bow in the glow of the morning sun they quickly awakened and joined them. Many of the people had seen that Timothy tended to stand back from the others. They had noticed he watched and did not get involved. They had also noticed that he did not praise God as one would expect him to, especially one who was going to Jerusalem to sacrifice.

They were so glad to see that he was finally fully praising God with his entire heart and being. Although no one had made mention of the fact before, they were all overjoyed at the change that had come about and they were glad they could praise God together.

Chapter 23

The little band of people on the boat were joined as one unified group. Together they would gather and worship and praise God. They were in complete unison now, working together, praising together, and helping each other. It was a little bit of heaven on earth.

One day Timothy thought he had seen Ross in the midst of the crowd. They had all been gathered around Meyer's Scriptures, well Timothy's now. They were reciting and finding verses to praise God with, to elevate their praise and joy on this journey as they should.

Timothy thought he had seen Ross nodding his head and smiling at the fact that Timothy was participating and taking part with the group. He would offer suggestions of Scriptures to read or share his thoughts on what some verses meant. He would praise with the rest of them. He had truly learned to give God praise. He studied the Word every moment he got during the day and the night. When he walked the lamb, he memorized verses, while the lamb ate he read and while the lamb rested he studied. Day after day this continued as he became more familiar with the Scriptures and more knowledgeable about how great his God is.

Timothy knew that he would be able to return to his father and his family and let them know that they had nothing to fear, Timothy understood, enough for now, and was growing and becoming closer to God as he continued to study.

"Look here," one man said from the edge of the group, "I found this earlier this morning and was so amazed by it." He stood up and tried to get into the center of the group, his eyes lit with excitement. "'For God, who said, "Light shall shine out of darkness," is the One who has shone in our hearts to give the Light of the knowledge of the glory of God in the face of Christ.'[159] It's true, isn't it? He is here now, shining in the darkness. It may not be night or dark with evil as in ages past, but He is still shining. He is shining from our hearts. Amazing, how bright a light it must be to be seen even in the day. It is such a pure and bright light. I am so glad that He shines in our hearts. I'm so glad that He is a part of us and we can worship Him."

A chorus of "Yes! Yes!" and "Praise God!" reverberated through the group. It was evident, internally and externally. Each person literally radiated with light. Each person sang praise and each person participated in giving God the glory.

Throughout these sessions of continual praise Timothy was never far from his lamb. The quickly growing lamb was as close to him as his shadow in the bright sun. He never roamed far and was always calm and easy going. It was as if he was joining in praise with the group, even though he couldn't talk or sing. In a way, he knew what was going on and wanted to be a part of the praise service to his King too.

Timothy would often subconsciously rub the little lamb and show it care as it sat beside him while he studied or talked. He felt like he was really growing. He understood more about God and he had come to agree that this idea of him travelling to Jerusalem was an excellent part of his life. He was glad that his father had asked that he go and that Ross had guided him in that decision. It hadn't made all that he had been through easy, but he was glad because it brought about a needed change in his life and it helped him to understand the Lord better.

Sometimes he still had apprehensive feelings. There were times when he was away from Peter or Meyer or the others on the boat, lying by himself on his bunk, when he would occasionally question whether or not he really could do the task before him. But when those times came up, he pulled out that piece of paper that Ross had given him and reread it. "You will keep him in perfect peace, whose mind is stayed on You, because he trusts in You."[160] It would help to bring him comfort and help him to realize that he was exactly where God wanted him to be. Taking care of his lamb and singing praises to his Lord.

Chapter 24

Timothy had packed his belongings hours before. They were sitting at his feet, with the lamb right beside his leg. He was not so little anymore, but more precious than ever. Timothy had spent much time with him on the boat ride. He had taken care to feed him and see that all his needs were met. He had carefully inspected him daily to be sure that no injury had come to him. Many times in the evenings he would sit on deck with the lamb, Word of God in hand learning more about the one true God whom he served.

    Today they would be leaving the boat. He, Peter, Meyer, the lamb, and the dozens of others that were on board were planning on finishing the last part of their journey to Jerusalem on foot. They had had a tremendous time together. He would have memories of them singing and praising together day and night for the rest of his life. His new discovery along with their fellowship made Timothy feel as if he would float all the way to the city for the remainder of the trip. He was glad that their time together was not coming to an end, but that he could continue to enjoy such blessings for the next few days.

He now stood on deck, straining to see what he could of the land. His mind remained focused, his thoughts taken captive to those of the Lord. This time he was not inspecting the plants and comparing them with those he had grown at home. He was not even looking to see new varieties of plants that he could get cuttings from to take home with him. No, this time the only reason he wanted to see any vegetation at all was to see the "works of the LORD,"[161] so he could praise God for His handiwork.

As they approached the shoreline Timothy could, for the first time, really see the land that led to Zion. The colors and plants were amazing. Everything was its full vibrant color and size. Each plant had striven to do its best to bring glory to God. As far as Timothy's eyes could see the beauty of God's creation stretched before him, in its fullness.

"O mountains of Israel, you shall shoot forth your branches and yield your fruit to My people Israel."[162] His eyes quickly jumped to a small group of people who were walking by the water. He was astonished to notice how bright their faces were. So much brighter than others he had seen. They passed, and his eyes once again went back to absorbing all of the plant life that covered the land. Surely it was true what they had said, His branches did yield fruit, such beautiful and amazing fruit.

Timothy stared for what felt like hours, before Peter finally broke his reverie. "Come on, this is only the beginning. You will see far greater still, the closer you get to the city. Then, the best of all, God Himself upon the throne! Let's go." Peter didn't hesitate, but with the others quickly exited the boat. There was great anticipation and excitement in their steps. They were nearly there.

Timothy picked up the lamb and his belongings, moving in robotic motions without too much thought. His brain was stunned from the beauty and his lips were parted in awe at what he could see. If the path were to get better than this, there was no way that Timothy could imagine it or describe it, for what he saw now amazed him.

It was still another eight days travel until they reached Zion. Peter had told Timothy that the land from here to the city would be nearly flat, but then it would rise once they got there, until they saw the peak, which was Zion. It was the highest point, so was therefore easily noticed, aside from some other obvious details, but Peter didn't expand on those, actually, no one did.

The group headed up the trail, beginning the many days' journey into the city. Some sang a low praise song, some quoted Scriptures, others, amazed as Timothy, walked on in awe of God and His goodness.

As he continued closer to Jerusalem Timothy noticed his surroundings. He saw the fields. They no longer had the same pull on him that they once did, but that did not lessen their beauty. They were utterly captivating, more vibrant, more luscious then he had ever seen before. Timothy had thought his crops were wonderful, but these, these were stunning. A land flowing with milk and honey,[163] as described in the Old Testament, now poured with prosperity in their crops and their land. It was beyond what Timothy could ever have imagined, as if the land itself was offering praise.[164] So he stopped and was sure to offer up his praise and thanks to the grand Creator and Father of the earth, the One whose "works" these really belonged to and the One who truly deserved the praise.

Chapter 25

After two days of awe and amazement at what Timothy had seen they finally stopped to rest for the Sabbath. The group had increased in size and volume each day.[165] The roads were crowded and along the sides of the road were people walking and resting. It felt as if he were part of a herd of sheep, being gathered and led.[166] Perhaps they were. They were on their way to their Shepherd. Others were coming and saying, "Let us go speedily to pray before the LORD, and to seek the LORD of hosts."[167] And so they continued, offering praises both day and night. Timothy could barely tell the difference between old timers who had been coming for years and new comers who were on their journey for the first time. Everyone joined in praising whenever they knew the psalm, or they just listened in agreement when they didn't. One thing was for sure, he was enjoying it.

Meyer and Peter still spent the majority of their time with him, but they also had other friends that joined them. They really were impressive men, so vibrant and excited about going to see God. Timothy was still unsure at times if he was really ready. He wasn't sure what to expect when he got there, but he knew that following God and serving Him was his best choice. So he continued, trying to do the best he could with the limited knowledge he had. Sometimes he would stray away from the crowd, trying to fall back or stay on the edge and just enjoy the sheer beauty of the earth, but with so many people travelling there was soon becoming no "back" of the crowd. The people stretched on for miles, as did their smiles, songs, encouragement, and praise.

Many families had booths along the road set up with food for the travelers. Since there were limited places to sit, most took their meal or fruit and walked with it. The booths were covered with fresh fruits and vegetables. This was most definitely the land of plenty.

Today, since it was the Sabbath there would be no walking. The group had found an alcove on the side of the road, where they could rest for the day. There were fruit trees nearby, they had picked the fruit they wanted the night before. Today they were to rest, sing and praise God. Timothy used this time to reflect on all he had seen and learned on his journey so far and to spend some time with his lamb. He had read that the Lord was like a lamb, he had come to be the sacrifice. Timothy had tried to list some of the character traits that he could see in the lamb that he thought would be most like God's. He could see kindness, caring, patience and contentment for sure. He knew these were some of the character traits that he too ought to exercise in order to become more like the true Lamb. As he stroked his lamb he thought about how he could demonstrate that character in himself.

"Hi, Timothy. I can imagine you are thoroughly enjoying this view. Just wait until you get to Jerusalem, it will be so much more amazing than this."

Timothy turned his head. He could see the glow of light out of the left corner of his eye. He turned to see Ross standing under a tree. He got up, left the lamb and walked over. The question was on his face, but nothing came out of his mouth.

"How is it going?"

"Well, thanks. I was just thinking about this lamb. He's been quite amazing on the journey. I thought he would be terrible to care for, but he's been easy. I often find myself looking at him and asking him how he is. I want to be sure he's comfortable and well cared for. I've grown fond of this little guy. I see in him traits that I want to have in me."

"God's lambs are always so precious. That is why He chose them for the sacrifice. They are a great example of what He was willing to give for everyone. They are so meek and humble. This lamb is content to give you his all, as you should want God to have your all. I've seen a change in you. I'm glad, continue praising God. It is your willingness to obey Him that is worth so much to God. He will be pleased with your sacrifice."

The thought caused Timothy to pause. He knew the purpose of carrying the lamb. At first he couldn't wait to be rid of it. He felt like it demanded so much attention and time. He wasn't ever certain how to tell if it was okay or if it needed more food or water or anything. It had been frustrating at first. The thought occurred to him that it might not have been the lamb that was so frustrating; it could just have been his being upset with having to go on this journey. Unfortunately the lamb suffered because of it. But now he had grown quite fond of the lamb and wasn't sure what it was going to be like having to give it up.

His thoughts were interrupted by Ross again. "Are you ready for Jerusalem?" The question was loaded, it meant more than just the walk there or giving up the lamb, he knew it was directed towards his heart.

He paused while stroking the lamb before he answered. "Ready? Ready to walk there, yes. Ready to give up the lamb. I guess so. It might be a bit hard, I've grown used to his company." He took a deep breath. "Ready to give him as a sacrifice. I think so. I know I must obey. I know offering a sacrifice and praise is the right thing. I know God is the true God and worthy of worship. I know there is no other way and I am glad to do this. I have learned many praise psalms and Scriptures about God. I want to obey all His commandments. I'm just concerned that He might not accept me. What if, even when I go, He takes one look at me and rejects my offering. What if He says, 'No, I still see doubt there, you've been rejected.' Then what? I don't want to fake it, but how do I know it's real, how can I say the action of praise is the same as praise that seems to bubble and spill over in these people? What if it's still not enough?"

Ross sat and listened to all of Timothy's concerns. They were some real fears that he was having. There was no doubt about that. He should be concerned, because grave were the consequences if he did not have a true heart, if indeed, he tried to fake it. Ross also knew that Timothy didn't really understand what sacrifice was. Yes, it was to give up something, but Timothy had never seen death before, so he knew it was going to be difficult for him to watch life exit this innocent lamb. "Do you believe God is good?"

"Yes, look around. How could such beauty exist if He were not good? And the Scriptures say, 'that all things work together for good to those who love God, to those who are the called according to *His* purpose.'"[168]

"Then trust Him. Continue to take one step forward at a time. Do as He asked you to. Don't depend just on emotions or circumstances, trust Him. Surrender your intellect, your emotions and your will[169] and respond to His goodness. Keep walking, walking is a part of worship."

"If only it were so easy."

"He did not promise easy, but He did promise never to abandon you.[170] He will guide you, just call on Him[171] and take the next step. It's a promise."

With that Ross disappeared. He left Timothy alone with his thoughts, but not alone for he had a peace within him. It was as if he knew everything was going to be alright. The thought crossed Timothy's mind that he should have asked about the welfare of his family, but it was too late now.

"Not my emotions? They shouldn't be in control, easier said than done." Timothy told his lamb. "Well," he said as he motioned for the lamb to join him, "let's obey. Take a step forward. Shall we join those who are already praising?" The little lamb seemed to nod as he stood. Timothy smiled briefly, as if realizing he just asked a lamb a question, but more surprisingly was he also got an answer.

Timothy spent the rest of the day singing and listening to praises. He prayed a silent prayer often throughout the day, "Please Lord, make this real in my heart."

Chapter 26

The next few days were a continuous song service of praise. It did help to raise one's spirits to constantly be around such uplifting music and thoughts. The noise was overwhelming, almost deafening, but not at all harmful to the ears.[172] The days were also filled with sharing and memorizing scripture, singing and taking care of the lamb. As they travelled Timothy noted the increased beauty. Everything, from the largest tree to the tiniest blade of grass to the littlest pebble, it was all magnificent.[173] Each gave its all, each looked its best for the King.

The landscape continued to change as they walked. "Beautiful, isn't it?" Peter queried, but he didn't wait for a response. "For water will break forth in the wilderness and streams in the Arabah. The scorched land will become a pool and the thirsty ground springs of water; …and the ransomed of the LORD will return and come with joyful shouting to Zion, with everlasting joy upon their heads. They will find gladness and joy, and sorrow and sighing will flee away."[174]

Trees lined the sides of the deep river that stretched across the land. The river, located on the east side, was filled with fish, jumping and swimming. The trees were bright and loaded with ripe fruit. Many creatures swarmed around the fresh water and various colored birds flew from tree to tree.[175] In the distance Timothy could see hills. They were round and soothing, coated in grass and spotted trees. However, the present beauty of the land as they walked kept him in awe so his eyes did not often stray to the horizon. When they did however he noticed that the sun always seemed to be shining brightly from that direction. It made it difficult to see what was really ahead, so he stayed focused on the land nearby as well as the increasing number of people and the activities around him.

About a two days walk outside the city there were fields of palm trees. The land was riddled with them. It seemed like they were growing for miles upon miles, beautiful palms with branches hanging low. Their rate of growth must have increased recently as Timothy notice a large amount of branches on the ground beneath the trees. It looked like a soft bed of palms awaiting the arrival of one who needed rest.

Timothy noticed some people picking up the fronds as they walked. He knew they would need them for their covering of their sukkot; he would too, and he was a bit concerned with how he could carry his supplies, the palm branches, and the lamb. He should not have worried though, there were plenty of people who were more than happy to help him out by carrying a few extra palms each.

As he looked around that afternoon, he thought they all must look a sight. There were dozens of people walking the 'Highway of Holiness'[176] on their way to Zion, ready to march up a hill with a few supplies on their backs and palm fronds stuffed under their arms and waving to and fro above their heads. In the mix was Timothy carrying his little lamb, making sure he was protected through all of the activity.

Timothy also noticed that the closer they got to the city, the brighter the days and nights became. He had thought about asking someone about this, but since everyone was praising and singing nonstop he thought it might not be an appropriate question to ask as they neared the city. Somehow, someway, he had to focus his mind on what he needed to do and not let it get sidetracked with the 'what ifs' or the whys as there were some things that he wasn't sure about.

Chapter 27

Timothy woke up the last morning of his journey to sounds of Scripture being recited. Straining his ears to hear amidst the trees was not enough for him, so he quickly gathered his things and the lamb and headed in the direction of the recitation.

> "Give the king Your judgments, O God,
> And Your righteousness to the king's son.
> May he judge Your people with righteousness
> And Your afflicted with justice.
> Let the mountains bring peace to the people,
> And the hills, in righteousness.
> May he vindicate the afflicted of the people,
> Save the children of the needy
> And crush the oppressor.
> Let them fear You while the sun *endures*,

And as long as the moon, throughout all generations.
May he come down like rain upon the mown grass,
Like showers that water the earth.
In his days may the righteous flourish,
And abundance of peace till the moon is no more.
May he also rule from sea to sea
And from the River to the ends of the earth.
Let the nomads of the desert bow before him,
And his enemies lick the dust.
Let the kings of Tarshish and of the islands bring presents;
The kings of Sheba and Seba offer gifts.
And let all kings bow down before him,
All nations serve him.
For he will deliver the needy when he cries for help,
The afflicted also, and him who has no helper.
He will have compassion on the poor and needy,
And the lives of the needy he will save.
He will rescue their life from oppression and violence,
And their blood will be precious in his sight;
So may he live, and may the gold of Sheba be given to him;
And let them pray for him continually;
Let them bless him all day long.
May there be abundance of grain in the earth on top of the mountains;
Its fruit will wave like *the cedars of* Lebanon;
And may those from the city flourish like vegetation of the earth.
May his name endure forever;
May his name increase as long as the sun *shines*;
And let *men* bless themselves by him;
Let all nations call him blessed.
Blessed be the Lord God, the God of Israel,
Who alone works wonders.
And blessed be His glorious name forever;
And may the whole earth be filled with His glory.
Amen, and Amen."[177]

It had been recited as a prayer, a prayer of thanksgiving to the King for fulfilling His promises. The peace which they spoke of resided in this place. The mountains were a comfort, but the mountain, the tallest mountain, the mountain of mountains where the house of the LORD was,[178] was where peace resided and where the peace on earth came from.

Timothy felt a sprig of joy begin to take root within him. It seemed to course through his body, flowing through his veins, causing his legs to press forward. He felt a need to get to the city. The joy began to spread across his face and into his eyes. "It isn't going to be much longer." Timothy thought, "I will be there soon. I will see the King. I must see the King. All of this beauty, everything I have seen comes from Him. I must praise Him." The thoughts consumed him and took over the movement of his body.

His pace increased along with the others around him. No one was pushing or shoving, but everyone was so excited to be so near the city. They were ecstatic to be able to be there and offer their praise to God. This feast was going to be the best one they had ever been too.

Somehow through the course of the day Timothy was separated from Meyer and Peter and from many of the others he had travelled with since the boat ride. By the evening no one he knew or had met could be seen. He was travelling in a sea of unknown faces, and yet, he felt comfortable, as if he had known them his entire life. Timothy felt no fear or worry. He would miss his friends' company and he wished for one more opportunity to talk with them and thank them, but he knew what his purpose was and he knew that he must keep his mind focused to see that purpose through. He must praise. He must give worship. He must stand before the King.

Ross and Tearle sat down in New Jerusalem by the river. They had come together to work on a plan or schedule for meeting with Timothy while he was in the city. They didn't want to bombard him with their presence, but they did want to be there when he needed them. After deciding their times they sat overlooking the river. It was so clear and clean. It glimmered brightly, just like

Quest for a True Heart

the clear streets of gold behind them. The grass was perfect and the homes magnificent.

After a while Ross broke the silence. "Amazing isn't it? You know, I never could have imagined this while I lived on earth. And I never get tired of looking at it now either."

"Yeah, the brilliance and beauty are just breath taking, but it is God's glory that shines through each level that makes it so amazing."

"Do you remember when we received our rewards at the Judgment Seat of Christ?"[179]

"Oh yes, it was like it was yesterday. We stood in line, it appeared to be so long, but it wasn't. It was as if we were before the King in an instant. I knew that our works would be examined; only those done for Christ would last.[180] I knew we would have to give an account of our life, a report.[181] *I* had always dreamed of hearing Him say, 'Well done, good and faithful servant.' I thought I had lived well, done my best."

"Yes, but I felt so humbled before Him. His presence was perfect and pure. My life looked so insignificant. Was the life I lived enough to count for Christ? Could any of my works, any of the things I did on earth make it through? I wondered if there really would be treasure in heaven for me. I had only lived a few short years on earth, had I made the best use of them that I could?[182] Did I demonstrate His character, His likeness and fruit to everyone I came in contact with? But as He who is faithful has promised,[183] there were rewards waiting for me.[184] The people whose lives I was blessed to touch on earth were my treasures for God.[185] He gave me a crown of rejoicing,[186] so grateful am I that I could impact their lives and they too could be here. I praise Him for His mercy and His grace. He forgave me for everything that burned up, many things that I thought would count, but did not add anything to His kingdom, yet, there were other things that counted instead, things I never realized.[187] He gave me a reward far greater than I deserved. I have been so blessed serving Him over the territories that He has assigned to me.[188] I had an influence on a few on earth then, now I have a great many in the territories.[189] God is so good that I can use my crowns to serve Him further still. My crown of glory[190] and righteousness[191] are gifts I use to serve Him. What a privilege to bring Him further glory!"

Tearle nodded his head in agreement, the gratitude and praise clearly showed on his face. "Isn't it so true? He has given us great gifts, both young and old on earth. When in truth we deserved punishment. Isn't it amazing, we came to Him in all His glory, light radiating from the throne,[192] stronger than the sun and I bowed before Him. The contrast between us was so great, but instead of condemnation and punishment, He offered forgiveness. He took of what was useful to Him, to build on His foundation and burned the rest away.[193] I felt such great sorrow to see so much of my life gone, wasted, but I was grateful that there was some left for Him. He too gave me the crown of rejoicing and I am glad to offer Him praise every day. I can rejoice with those in the city and those on earth. We celebrate together. He also gave me the crown of life[194] for remaining faithful until death. My life on earth was short. Not even 30 years. It was ended while I took a stand for God. He has been faithful, to reward His servant. There were and are no regrets for what I have done. There were so many people who were watching my death, I did not know what happened to them, but I had hoped that they turned and believed in God when they saw my death. I have since learned that many came to Him and I was rewarded for it because of my faithfulness. How humbling to think the Almighty God would honor me for such an act."

"He does. He misses nothing His servants do. He blesses us and gives us responsibilities to continue to work with His people."

"Praise the LORD!
Praise God in His sanctuary;
Praise Him in His mighty expanse.
Praise Him for His mighty deeds;
Praise Him according to His excellent greatness.

> Praise Him with trumpet sound;
> Praise Him with harp and lyre.
> Praise Him with timbrel and dancing;
> Praise Him with stringed instruments and pipe.
> Praise Him with loud cymbals;
> Praise Him with resounding cymbals.
> Let everything that has breath praise the LORD.
> Praise the LORD!"[195]

Their faces shone brighter as they praised God together, reflecting more of His glory. In the distance they could hear the sounds of the instruments and singing. The musicians and choir constantly played, offering praise. They too had an amazing job in serving their King. Everyone was satisfied with their reward, it was far beyond what any of them deserved. Each resurrected saint was so grateful that they could serve God in the capacity that He had designed them to serve. What joy! What harmony! What unity! What perfection!

With a deep sigh of satisfaction Ross bid his farewell. "I had better go and check on Timothy. We'll keep in touch. Keep praising!" and with that the men were gone.[196]

Chapter 28

It was not much farther now, he could see the mountain on which Jerusalem stood. The highest point in the land,[197] it was as if all the land on earth paid homage to the city, by lowering itself to its Majesty. He looked around the horizon and noticed beams of rainbows cascading across the hills. They were everywhere. They added to the iridescent colors and beauty of the already magnificent land. The clouds too were rainbows of color, just as magnificent as anything he had ever seen. Just when Timothy didn't think it could get any more wonderful, here he stood in awe again. His heart was thrilled and he just wanted to rejoice,[198] so he did.

"I will 'praise the name of the LORD [my] God, who has dealt wondrously with'[199] me.

> 'Praise the name of the LORD; Praise *Him*, …
> Praise the LORD, for the LORD *is* good;
> Sing praises to His name, for *it is* pleasant. ..

> For I know that the LORD *is* great,
> and our Lord *is* above all gods.
> Whatever the LORD pleases He does,
> in heaven and in earth,'[200]
> 'Oh, give thanks to the LORD, for *He is* good!
> For His mercy *endures* forever.
> Oh, give thanks to the God of gods!
> For His mercy *endures* forever.
> Oh, give thanks to the Lord of lords!
> For His mercy *endures* forever.'[201]
> 'Blessed be the LORD out of Zion, who dwells in Jerusalem!'[202]

His praise continued as he approached the city. The closer he got the better he could see an enormous cube that hovered over the earthly city of Jerusalem.[203] It was like a canopy,[204] protecting the earth beneath. It provided the protection from above, as well as the light from the King.[205] Timothy could tell it was Zion, Ross's home. The walls glistened – almost as if they were crystal, yet shiny like transparent gold. The light that shone from the city was brighter and purer than any light he had ever seen before, when it shone through the walls and foundation it exploded into streams of rainbows that covered the entire area. It gave the hills an aura that simply awestruck a person and demanded praise. There was simply no other way to explain it. He could see now why so few people had tried to discuss the land's appearance. There was nothing else in all the earth like it that could be compared or likened to it.

Timothy wondered where Ross might be. He had a knack for showing up, perhaps he was looking down through the walls of the city or maybe he was behind some of the trees or hidden in the crowds watching him from a distance.

As Timothy continued to look around he also noticed light coming from the city of Zion itself. He wasn't sure if the main light was coming from below where the LORD's throne was in Old Jerusalem or if it was shining down from above, from the throne of God in the New Jerusalem, the city of Zion.

The various colors of light streamed in all directions, lighting a clear path, even in the fading evening. Timothy continued to walk with the lamb close to him in the crowd of people around him. The lamb seemed eager and sure, as if he knew where to go. There was no hesitation in his step, but an anticipation to reach the city and see the One whom they came to worship, the One whom they'd travelled so far to see.

"Have you any idea what is about to happen to you? Do you know you are on your way to be slaughtered?" thought Timothy.

Timothy had grown so fond of the lamb over the past weeks. Could he really give this precious lamb to be sacrificed? In reality, Timothy didn't really know what that meant.

Palm branches swayed as everyone carried what they needed to make their tent, their sukkot. Timothy now carried his own branches, he only had a few since he had been separated from the others but he figured they would do. A Scripture passage came to mind as his palm branches swayed. Was it really so many years ago, Jesus, the Christ, the LORD, had walked this very same pathway? He too had headed to Jerusalem. How different it had been then. The landscape was different, the time was different, and the purpose was different, sort of. When Jesus had come people were waving palm branches,[206] were cheering, and were praising Him. They were thinking He was coming to take His rightful place on the throne in Jerusalem. Jesus simply rode in on a donkey, as prophesied.[207] He knew what was going to happen. He did not come to take over the world, but to capture people's hearts. Giving up His life showed just how great a love he had. Timothy knew a similar sacrifice would take place for the lamb. He knew he didn't fully understand it, but that was okay. He trusted God and knew what he had to do. He knew this was part of his praise.

Timothy glanced at the lamb again. There were still no hesitations in his steps. He kept on going, right to the city. Timothy, who had slowed his pace to take it all in, picked up his pace to keep up with the little lamb. "I wonder if you are not walking in as Jesus did, knowing full well what will meet you on the other side, but knowing that you have come to serve Your Father, to die. You walk in with anticipation, knowing the events that will occur will be for the glory[208] of God and the benefit of His people.

Even you lamb have purpose, have a job to do. The sad thing is that you recognized your purpose far more easily and willingly than I ever did. Well done faithful servant." He quit talking and bent down to pick up the lamb. He decided he would stay out here on the hillside and make camp, tomorrow he would finish his journey.

    The resurrected ladies encompassed the city of Jerusalem. The men had gone through earlier and had attended to roadways and logistics. The women continued their work by carrying food to different stands, hanging signs of praise, and cheerfully greeting the visitors as they flowed in. The city was abuzz with activity. The colored rays of rainbows danced around jumping from place to place, lighting the pathways and areas of the city. The surrounding grassy areas on the outskirts of the city was where the majority of the people would camp, they too danced with rainbows of color.
    Each resurrected saint walked around (seemingly floated around) with such joy. It was more than contagious. As each person came into contact with one another it was like their joy was magnified. It truly was an exciting and amazing time of year.

Chapter 29

Timothy managed to arrive on the 14th of Tishri, the streets and area were already crowded. The crowd began to veer off the path. Timothy knew that they would not all be able to fit in the city, it would be too crowded. He would have to make his tent for the week on a small slope[209] outside of the city and wait until morning to go in. He followed the crowd to the left of the path and continued up the slope. Rather than settling right in the middle of the crowd he decided to wander through and find a place on the edge. It almost seemed that one tent was upon another, and he wanted his space. He and his lamb were able to maneuver through the maze of people and tents. There were scattered trees here and there too, but when he reached the far side he found a small grove of trees. "Perfect," he thought. "What better place to rest than by His creation and recognize His greatness through it. It will be like looking from my past to my future, from the way I used to serve to the way I now serve."

Although Timothy was not familiar with construction, he did his best to make the simple shelter. He strung his blankets between the trees, covering three sides of his tent and used the palms for the roof. The palms stuck here and there. There were also holes all through the roof, but he didn't mind, besides, that's the way it was supposed to be.[210] His temporary home was not spacious or perfect, but it would do. The rays of light, the beams of rainbow, the glistening color from above added a beautiful color display day and night to his tent. He was more than happy to let it in.

The contrast from the life he had known to the light that emanated from Jerusalem was drastic. But the light wasn't the only difference he noticed. The vegetation here was so vibrant, so alive too. How terrible that he had thought his work so great and his garden so amazing before. Compared to this, well, the only contrast he could think of was how he first felt about Amos' land. But here, it was God's work and if Timothy had praised God more he knew there would have been a difference in his own gardens.

"No wonder people could praise the LORD so," Timothy spoke to his lamb. The picture before him was more than he could've dared to imagine, let alone put into words. If this was the drastic difference he could see, he could not fathom the difference his great grandfather had tried to explain. He recalled Amos' place, the worst thing he had ever seen, but that did not compare with some descriptions his grandfather told him of. It was no wonder his face always glowed, his words were always full of God's love and praise, and he seemed full of God's love. He saw the effect God had on the world. For Timothy to have just a piece of that reality was quite humbling.

> "Turn your eyes upon Jesus,
> Look full in His wonderful face,
> And the things of earth will grow strangely dim,
> In the light of His glory and grace."[211]

So the things of earth seemed to fade. What Timothy had held in highest regard, his love of plants, his life, and his desires no longer seemed to consume his heart. It began to dim in comparison to all the great wonders around him. But the greatest was yet to behold. Timothy could barely contain the excitement of getting to see the LORD in the city.

Tomorrow would be a holy convocation, a day of rest, where no work was to be done,[212] after that he would get to go into the city.

Timothy had purchased food supplies from the bountiful harvest a few hills back for today and part of the week. Instead of examining the fruit or the land he had spent most of his day in awe and amazement at God's handiwork. For the rest of the day he had listened to or joined in with others singing psalms. His journey here had been a memorable one, one that had changed his life. He couldn't wait to see what would happen next.

Before daybreak Timothy awoke to singing. It was a psalm.

> "O come, let us sing for joy to the LORD,
> Let us shout joyfully to the rock of our salvation.
> Let us come before His presence with thanksgiving,
> Let us shout joyfully to Him with psalms.
> For the LORD is a great God
> And a great King above all gods,
> In whose hand are the depths of the earth,
> The peaks of the mountains are His also.
> The sea is His, for it was He who made it,
> And His hands formed the dry land
> Come, let us worship and bow down,
> Let us kneel before the LORD our Maker.
> For He is our God.[213]

Timothy's heart soared as he joined in with the multitudes of others who were singing together[214] as they gathered around the city; the brilliant colors from the sky above, the exultant singing from the crowds, and the echo from hill to hill as the thousands that had gathered sang as one lifted Timothy's spirits and heart like never before. He was so privileged to be here and to be able to worship. He was so grateful that Ross had encouraged him along the way, even giving him a push when needed. He was also thankful for Peter and Meyer and Tearle who had all played a significant role in his trip. He was so grateful that he had not become a wayward wanderer.

Timothy decided to take a little walk later on that day. He could still hear the singing and praising in the background as he headed into the small alcove of trees, his lamb right by his side. The lamb had become a part of Timothy, a constant shadow, a companion, and an understanding friend. He was glad for his company and yet as his thoughts veered toward the future he thought that the journey back home might be lonely without him.

"I hope you weren't hoping for privacy," a voice said from behind him. "You don't find that much around here this time of year."

"Hi Tearle, it's nice to see you again."

"Likewise. Isn't it wonderful?" he asked as he pointed over the land around Jerusalem and Jerusalem itself. The view was really breathtaking. "I love this time of year. Actually, I don't know anyone who doesn't. It seems so right, so fitting you know, that the LORD has all of these people around Him worshipping and praising Him. He deserves it. I would love it if it were like this all the time."

"I think I'm beginning to understand what you mean. It has been so great being filled with praise and being around so many others who wish to praise God too. The air is electrified with everyone's energy. And," he paused for a moment, "I see it too, you know, why we should praise Him. You're right, look at this place! It's incredible! And I haven't even been in the city yet. I am overwhelmed and amazed at His works. I don't deserve to be a part of this."

"None of us do. Not the resurrected saints or the humans. It is only because of God's great love and mercy that any of us are here. Without Him, nothing would exist,[215] nothing would have any reason to exist. I am so glad that you are coming to see that now."

"Yes, I think I finally get it why my father and grandfather and great-grandfather are always praising Him. He deserves it. When you realize just how amazing He is, you can't help it, you have to praise Him."

"He sure does deserve our praise. Hey, be sure to mingle with some other people too, human and resurrected saints. Praise is always better in numbers. God made us to be together and to worship together."[216]

"Okay."

Timothy strolled slowly back to his tent. He gazed all around at the wonders he could see. At some points he closed his eyes and just listened to the music being carried across the air. There was peace and joy, but there was more than that too. There was love, grace, and mercy. It was all there. It was complete. There was nothing missing."

Timothy lay down in his makeshift tent, the lamb at his side, as he looked through the peep holes in the roof. Colored rays of light came in from the doorway as well. "Oh God, I am so grateful, you did not let me slip away. Thank you for sending your servants my way to guide me. Thank you for always taking care of me. Thank you for the company of this little lamb, it has been nice to have a constant source of love and companionship on this journey. 'O LORD, our Lord, How majestic is Your name in all the earth, Who [has] displayed Your splendor above the heavens!'"[217]

Timothy drifted off to sleep with praise on his lips and anticipation in his heart, tomorrow was now the day he was looking forward to, not dreading.

This was Louise's favorite time of year. She loved to serve and help out where she could. As a resurrected saint she had been placed in charge of overseeing the care of the visitors and travelers that had come and settled on the west side of Zion.[218] She would help see to their needs, along with the help of her young charge and many other assistants. The hospitality group was well organized. Different resurrected saints were responsible for different areas of the city. Louise had several saints working under her. They made sure each person was looked after and encouraged. Sometimes after a long journey some of the saints would be tired, but they wanted their energy to last, to thoroughly enjoy the magnificence of the city, but more importantly to be able to glorify the King of Kings as He should be glorified.

Louise and other resurrected saints spent days organizing food and making sure there were enough palm fronds for everyone to create sturdy tents during their stay. Their comfort was not as important as the time they would take to see and to praise the King, but these little things must be looked after.

Although Louise was not part of the musical group of resurrected saints, she never minded joining in their songs as they praised day and night throughout the city. Their voices reverberated and were joined by many people. It was as if Zion was an enormously large amphitheatre. The walls of the city reflected the sound which seemed to cause the city to rise to heaven on its own.

Chapter 30

The next morning Timothy heard many people rising and preparing to go to the temple in Jerusalem. Some called to each other from their tent, "Come, and let us go up to the mountain of the LORD, and to the house of the God of Jacob; and he will teach us of his ways, and we will walk in his paths: for the law shall go forth of Zion, and the word of the LORD from Jerusalem."[219]

Others would shout back, "Let us go."

The gates were always opened, ready to welcome visitors at any hour. The morning was already bright from the constant light that shone from the city as well as the rainbows of color shining all around the city.

Many people were reciting a psalm from of old. It was meant to give God praise, but it also told of their purpose for today.

> "Ascribe to the LORD the glory of His name;
> Bring an offering and come into His courts.

> Worship the Lord in holy attire;
> Tremble before Him, all the earth.
> Say among the nations, "The Lord reigns."[220]

Timothy's mouth moved to recite the passage as he prepared himself for the journey. He stepped outside his little palm branch tent to where the little lamb was. The lamb had been contentedly munching on grass while Timothy had been saying his own prayers and praises for the morning. "Let's have a look at you," Timothy said, bending down. He inspected the lamb, not one blemish, perfect, just as he knew it had to be in order for his lamb to be accepted. He had made it safely across the land. Together they were ready to go into Jerusalem and present themselves before the king.

He walked with his lamb in the direction of the temple. Timothy decided to carry it around his shoulders as the crowds thickened with people and animals all making their way to the gate. In his mind he thought it would be safer, but in his heart he wanted to be close to his friend during their last moments together.

As Timothy walked toward the city early that morning a song began in another area just outside the city. The sound travelled around until multitudes of people were singing praise. The sound echoed and reverberated, and was carried up from the low hills to the high mountain where the temple and the King awaited.

> "We bring the sacrifice of praise
> Unto the house of the Lord.
> We bring the sacrifice of praise
> Unto the house of the Lord.
> And we offer up to You
> The sacrifices of thanksgiving;
> And we offer up to You
> The sacrifices of joy."[221]

Their voices lifted to the heavens. It was so great that Timothy could physically feel himself ascending up the mountain with the music. It was as if he were floating toward the city and the temple, not walking with the lamb or struggling amongst the crowds. His heart was soaring and peace filled his being. With a tear in his eye he joined in the song the second time through, again stroking the head of his lamb.

Chapter 31

The gathering flowed as one. They wanted to be the first among the worshippers in the city. The group consisted mostly of men, a few had their children with them and even fewer brought their wives. Many of the people had an animal with them, one they had either brought with them on their journey, or one they had purchased nearby. A few people looked as if they would purchase their animal either on their way to the temple or another day during the week.

As Timothy looked across the sea of faces he noticed that every one of them expressed pure joy. With uplifted shining faces and brilliant smiles, they journeyed on. No one seemed lost or out of place. Timothy's excitement rose with the anticipation and the energy of those with whom he walked, yet, in the pit of his stomach still niggled a little fear and uncertainty.

The crowd travelled up the hill, leading toward the gate. Some chanted back and forth. "Lift up your heads, O gates, and be lifted up, O ancient doors, that the King of glory may come in! *Who is the King of glory?* The Lord strong and mighty, the Lord mighty in battle. Lift up your heads, O gates, and lift *them* up, O ancient doors, that the King of glory may come in! *Who is this King of glory?* The Lord of hosts, He is the King of glory."[222]

Others sang the ninety-sixth Psalm,

> "O sing unto the LORD a new song:
> sing unto the LORD, all the earth.
> Sing unto the LORD, bless his name;
> show forth his salvation from day to day.
> Declare his glory among the heathen,
> his wonders among all people.
> For the LORD *is* great, and greatly to be praised."

They were entering on the southeast side, through the royal gardens.[223] There was a trellis of colorful roses on either side. Cyclamen filled the landscape adding to the beauty of colors from above. The bright light from God shining through the foundation stones cast a glow over the Old city,[224] like multi-colored flood lights in each section. They gave a sense of warmth and care, a protective refuge to be in.

Timothy had heard of these gardens as a young child and had always wanted to see them, but somehow, even as overwhelmingly beautiful as they were; they didn't seem as important to him anymore. He held tightly to his lamb as he wove through the garden path. His focus was upward, the plants were to do their part and glorify God and Timothy was to do his. Not to be amazed at the plants, but to be amazed at God.

He continued walking along the path with the group. Many sang praises - Timothy just took it all in. It was so overwhelming, so amazing, so… he didn't know what to think about it.

He noticed within the crowd a variety of people, not just those prepared to sacrifice. The thought had never occurred to him that there might be other people there with purposes other than sacrificing to God or celebrating the Feast of Booths. He noted some ladies walking by, their smiles stretched across their faces and they appeared to be headed on a

Quest for a True Heart

great mission. Timothy could tell they were resurrected saints. The glow from their faces and the way they talked, praised, and encouraged others as they passed by could in no way confuse them with the humans before him who had also come to worship. "Hmm, they too have their purpose. They serve God, not by sacrificing at this time, but by serving His people," Timothy thought to himself.

As more visitors poured in, the resurrected saints continued to work. "Here are more, it is wonderful to see so many hearts turned toward God. He is certainly worthy!"

"Most definitely! You know, the Scriptures said this would happen. It says,

> They will come and shout for joy on the height of Zion,
> And they will be radiant over the bounty of the LORD—
> > Over the grain and the new wine and the oil,
> > And over the young of the flock and the herd;
> > And their life will be like a watered garden,
> > And they will never languish again."[225]

"That is so true. That is exactly what we see here. Oh, look! Here come some more! Let's go."

The two ladies hurried off to encourage, support, feed and care for the new visitors. They loved their job, seeing to the needs of those who came to Jerusalem. They were so glad they could serve their God in this way.

"Welcome visitors and children of the living God. Welcome to the city of the LORD![226] We are so glad that you have joined us this year. Put down your burden and get ready to praise, for He who is worthy is still on the throne!"[227]

"Would you like a roll sir?" a young resurrected saint asked him. "This will keep your strength as you journey to the temple. The line is long as the sacrificing begins today."

"Thank you kindly." Timothy took a roll, savoring his first bite as he watched her take her tray to the next person. The roll was delicious. It would keep him from being hungry, which was a good thing. He had been so focused on getting ready to join the crowd and enter Jerusalem that he had not carried any food for him or his lamb.

Timothy noticed that everything seemed to flow so smoothly and effortlessly here. There was peace, tranquility and a working together that he had never seen before. Even though the streets were crowded and there were so many extra people, there was no disorganization, no shouting, and no frustration. There was not even anyone explaining and telling everyone else what to do, it was so well laid out with everyone working smoothly together, that nothing seemed to cause any trouble, stress or difficulty. He decided to watch out for more evidences of this kind. To see how well the people and resurrected saints really functioned together in the city. He wanted to know if it was as amazing as Ross had told him. From what he could already see, it was as if they functioned as one unit.

After walking for nearly an hour Timothy could see the temple walls. He stopped right in place, mouth and eyes wide open. There were so many foreigners, so many people gathered to offer their sacrifices.[228] Timothy had never seen so many people. It would be many hours of waiting before he could get in the temple gates. He shifted the lamb on his shoulders and took a few steps forward.

Just ahead of him he could hear some men talking. They appeared to be a family, several generations who had come to worship together. "I was here when the temple was purified. It was many years ago. There was such sorrow and disgust that took place, but He came, He took His rightful place. It was like a refiner's fire. He got rid of all the impurities[229] all the bad and made this place His place, a good place. There is no purer gold, no better silver than the pureness that can be found here because of His presence. You can travel the world, but you will only find this here."

"Let us not forget," responded the middle aged looking one, "that it is not just the physical impurities he got rid of. There were many spiritual impurities as well as evil people who were here that were removed. We are so fortunate to be the ones who can come before Him and worship Him."

Timothy had never really thought about it before. But he guessed it was true. All of those who did not make it in this era were removed by

Him. Timothy wondered momentarily if he would have made it. Would his heart have been considered dedicated enough to God, or would he have been one of the ones that had been removed?

A conversation on the other side of him also caught his attention. "For years I have repeated the Shema, 'Hear, O Israel! The LORD is our God, the LORD is one! You shall love the LORD your God with all your heart and with all your soul and with all your might. These words, which I am commanding you today, shall be on your heart.'[230] Oh son, I want you to see their significance. Without God we are nothing. He made us and wants us to live for Him. If you serve Him with your life, do as He asks, you will live the best life that you can possibly live. Keep His words always with you, in your mind, memorize Scriptures, in your heart, live by what He teaches, with your hand write His words and with your lips proclaim His glory."

"Yes father," the young boy responded. He took in every word his father said. He wanted to please his father, he wanted to please God.

Timothy wished that his father would have brought him when he was younger. Perhaps if he had seen this before, perhaps if he had understood earlier he wouldn't have had this problem representing his family. Again he was filled with shame at the thought of how unworthy he really was.

The day passed quickly enough. There were many people milling around, many having their own conversations and many people willing to talk. As Timothy approached the temple he became even more apprehensive. "What am I doing here?" he thought. "How can I go and stand before God and offer this lamb, as great as He is and as poorly as I have lived for him." The thought crossed Timothy's mind to turn around. He could leave the city and just spend some more time in his palm tent, then he could think of what he would do next.

As he turned to leave he caught a glimpse of Ross. His face shone so brightly, as if he had just come from the presence of God Himself. Timothy thought he saw a slight shake of his head, as if in response to Timothy's thoughts. "No, no I can't turn back. I promised," he whispered to himself and took the next step forward, toward the temple.

"And the ransomed of the LORD will return and come with joyful shouting to Zion, with everlasting joy upon their heads. They will find gladness and joy, and sorrow and sighing will flee away.[231] Let's join in a song of praise!" It was a resurrected saint. He seemed to be on a nearby rooftop and had caught the attention of many in the waiting crowd. They were all pleased to join him. Timothy too joined in the song and his spirits began to lift.

Someone bumped into Timothy's arm and caught his attention. He had not noticed this person earlier in the crowd, but then again there were many faces.

"Oh, you know you are so fortunate." The man stated as he began a conversation with him.

"Yes, are you not as well?"

"Oh yes, I am. I am so glad God has blessed me. But my turn to live and make those choices are over, but you, my friend, you can still make many choices to serve God as He deserves."

Timothy realized the man was a resurrected saint. "Why? What was your life like? Do you not feel like you served Him well enough?"

"Oh, I do not wish to discuss that, for I did not live for my God, but myself, while I was alive.[232] It was not until I was close to death that I accepted Christ. He saved me. He forgave me and has given me the gift of life. That I can serve Him now is such a blessing. I, so undeserving. He, so great. What love He has. I am so grateful."

"You are a resurrected saint? Do you have a territory that you rule over? Is that how you serve now?"

"Oh no!"

"Don't all resurrected saints get territories to serve over?"

"Oh no, God rewards accordingly, depending on how we served Him when we lived on earth. Like I said, I did not live for Him, yet, he chose to let me reign with him and serve Him in His kingdom anyway."

"Are you not upset that you didn't get a territory? What about your reward? Your place? Did you get anything?"

"No, no territory. No crowns. I am just so grateful that I can serve my Lord here, now. He has forgiven me and washed away all my sins. I am glad that He accepted me. I cannot go back and change how I lived, but I can serve Him to my fullest capacity now. That is why I am here, I just love to walk with those going to the Temple, the anticipation is electrifying and the praise stupendous! Although it is greatest at this time of year, it really never stops. You know, no one just sails[233] through this city, whoever comes, for however long they come, they reside here. Whether it is only for a week or two, it is home. I hope you feel it too. You are home."

They continued to walk together. Timothy contemplating on the fact that the resurrected saints were not rewarded equally[234] and yet they were home, content to live with Christ in Zion. How they had lived and served during their life affected how they could serve in the Millennium. Timothy wondered if it would be the same for him. Although he lived during the Millennium, he wanted to be sure that he lived for God and did not have the same regrets that this man had. How terrible it would be not to want to think about any of your life because it had not been lived out for God. How horrible that everything you had ever done had simply burned up and you had nothing left to offer before the King. Timothy knew he did not want that same outcome. He wanted his life to count. He wanted to have gifts to offer to the King, gifts that would last and be worth something to Him, not that would burn up and mean nothing and be nothing.

The gates of the temple finally came into view. The walls were tall and light brown. They rose high above the ground, declaring their superiority as they looked down on the streets below. Timothy felt so small and insignificant. Those walls demanded respect and proclaimed that something special happened behind them. The gates were pushed wide open, welcoming everyone in. People were gathered, lined up with their animal, and prepared to offer a sacrifice. Amongst the singing and the talking Timothy could also hear the lowing of sheep and cattle as they too walked toward the temple. Everything and everyone flowed through the gates like a gentle brook being pushed along the course that it was designated to take.

Chapter 32

The day had been long, but filled with wonder. Timothy had learned a lot from just observing. The sheer magnificence of the city on Mount Zion[235] was more than he could possibly ever describe. The unity of the people was another awe amazing fact. Everyone just worked as one. Even with so many people, everything flowed. And the people he was able to listen to and talk to, well, they too had left an impression on him. Only what he did for Christ would last. His gardens would be of value if he worked them as a service to God. The way he could benefit the lives of others and turn them to God, that would last, but his working for selfish reasons, well, if he continued on that path he would have nothing.

Timothy knew he wanted to serve God. He had come with his little lamb to do so. A gentle, cool breeze swept across the hill as he took his final steps toward the gate. The breeze gave him energy and kept up his hopes, it wasn't too late.

Being the first day of sacrificing during the feast, after the day of rest, he knew the priests had already been busy offering the congregational offerings. It was required that thirteen bulls, two rams, and fourteen male lambs, each a year old with no defects, be sacrificed with their grain offering. Also, one male goat was offered for a sin offering of the people. All through the rest of the day people would come with their burnt offerings and with their grain and drink offerings.[236] It would be continual throughout the week, each day sacrifices being offered to God.

The sacrificing had started early. The Levitical priests[237] were dressed in their usual white linen garments. To the left was the altar. Because of the crowd he could see the fire rising from the top of the altar, but he did not get a good look at what was happening merely feet in front of him.

Just ahead of him he could hear the restlessness of the people. As they sang Timothy looked in the distance and saw people with their eyes closed, tears streaming down their cheeks. The music touched their souls, in turn they did what came natural, they thanked God inwardly while praising Him outwardly, but they were overjoyed with the thought of it all, while their animal was taken and offered as a burnt offering. Timothy stepped forward, getting a better look at the priests and the scene before him. Their faces puzzled Timothy. He stared at them nearly in disbelief. They seemed to be enjoying their job. They worked with smiles of contentment. They did not look exhausted from the work they had already accomplished today. They spoke calmly to the people in line, encouraging their decisions and saying praises to God. Timothy held onto the little lambs legs. He had become accustomed to them being around his neck. He loved to hold the lamb and feel its warmth and comfort. This lamb had been with him for his entire journey. It had seen all that Timothy had and been through each experience with him. Timothy was afraid he would soon feel empty without the lamb.

The priests worked diligently. In no time he was at the front of the line, being greeted. "Welcome, may I see your sacrifice."

Timothy carefully took the lamb and placed it on the ground for the priest to examine. Timothy still held on to the lamb, as if he thought it might run away, but he knew it wouldn't, he just couldn't bear to let it go completely. It had been through so much with him.

"This sacrifice you offer to God, comes from you and your family?" the priest questioned.

"Yes, we offer it with all our hearts. We seek to obey and follow all of God's statutes that He has outlined for our lives."

"And keep the charge of the Lord your God: to walk in His ways, to keep His statutes, His commandments, His judgments, and His testimonies, as it is written in the Law of Moses, that you may prosper in all that you do and wherever you turn?"[238]

Timothy nodded his head, "Yes."

"Your animal is accepted.[239] As Hezekiah once prayed, 'May the good Lord provide atonement for everyone *who* prepares his heart to seek God, the Lord God of his fathers.'[240] Let us offer him now before the King of Kings."

Timothy noticed that the brightness of the area increased. The colors glowing from above seemed to dull in the brilliance of the light that now was. It seemed to brighten everything. He wasn't sure what caused it.

Timothy looked at the lamb as it was taken away, now accepted by the priest at the temple.

The priest wasted no time. He took a knife and with one swipe, the little lamb, his companion on this long journey, was dead. Its blood, which was bright and fresh and warm, flowed from his neck and was caught in a bowl. It flowed quickly and easily. This little lamb who had done nothing but follow him and show its dedication, was gone. Gone because of him and his lack of love for Christ. This lamb died for him. Died as Christ.

The words of a song came to him as he watched the blood drain from the animal. Tears welled up in his eyes as his lips unconsciously mouthed the words of the song.

> See, from his head, his hands, his feet,
> sorrow and love flow mingled down.
> Did e'er such love and sorrow meet,
> or thorns compose so rich a crown.

> Were the whole realm of nature mine,
> that were an offering far too small;
> love so amazing, so divine,
> demands my soul, my life, my all.[241]

It was the first time Timothy had ever seen death, had seen the end of a life. All he had ever seen that was lifeless was Jacan. He remembered what the lack of life looked like, but he had never seen life disappearing, life dying, no longer existing, ending right before his eyes. There was a deep pain in his stomach, a sick feeling. He couldn't describe it nor had he ever experienced it before. His thoughts rushed together, causing him to feel dizzy. He wasn't sure he could watch any more as his lifeless lamb was carried away. He was devastated. How could this bring such joy to people? How could it possibly be their favorite time of the year? How could this make them sing praises to God Most High? Something that was so opposite of what the King stood for – for life, goodness, care, love? It went completely against everything he had ever learned. Why this death? Why?

The milling crowd seemed to disappear, the sounds of the crowd and the animals faded. Timothy stumbled, barely able to walk; such were the hurricane of thoughts in his head. They completely set him off balance. He groped for the walls, anything to help him steady himself. As he reached out he glimpsed at his arms. Empty. Arms that had been full, carrying a little life for weeks, were now empty. There was nothing to fill them with nothing to replace what was gone.

He managed to make it to the gate – he stumbled and bumped into a man. It was Meyer whom he had not seen since they were parted when they neared the city.

"Timothy, it's so great to see you again. Oh, what a day!" he lowered his head to look at Timothy, stopping his string of praises to God. "Timothy, are you okay?" he asked, genuinely concerned.

Timothy could barely shake his head as he stumbled out of the gate. "I can't…I don't…" he couldn't get the words out. The pit, the sick feeling in his stomach was coming up and choking him. He just couldn't understand.

Meyer grabbed his arm to steady him, "Come," he directed as he led Timothy down the path and to a street Timothy was unfamiliar with.

Chapter 33

Timothy wasn't sure how far they walked. He followed him, or was pulled along by him. They ended at a little house. It was square, made of mud bricks. The furnishings were simple, but comfortable. Timothy sat down in one of the chairs and took the drink offered to him by a woman.

Timothy looked up and tried to mumble a thank you, but nothing came out.

"I'm…I'm…" Timothy tried again, "How? Why?"

"Your sacrifice – your lamb," understanding was dawning on Meyer. "Think of the great loss and misunderstanding you feel. Think of all that doesn't make sense now. Then think of God. He is perfect and demands a high standard, but the love He has for you and me drives Him to take drastic measures. For us now a lamb, but it is to remind us of a far greater sacrifice, a sacrifice no one could ever understand. For you a sweet lamb, for God, He gave His one and only perfect Son. The Son whom He loved.

For us unloving. imperfect, terrible people He came to die. Death, evil, pain, all that is terrible; it was done – out of love."

The woman spoke. He noticed that she was a resurrected saint. "God's love to an individual can be seen in how He cares for details, he takes care of every little thing, each plant, each seed. He does not let any birds fall that He is not aware of. He sees they get fed." She continued, "I see His faithfulness in the seasons of the year, they are consistent and they always come, just like we always know that the sun rises. He sent His only Son to pay the price for our sin and our wrong, since that is worthy of death and has been since the Garden of Eden. He did this so we could be with Him, it proves His love for us. Because of His great love shown then and continued on, even now, it means that I want to spend time to know more about God. He is the One who made it possible for us spend eternity with Him. I want to do what would please Him. I want to serve Him. This sacrifice is what He asked for. Not to be cruel or to make it easy, but because it is a reminder of His great love for us. He doesn't want us to forget it, ever. So this is a good reminder to show how serious He is about us, about you. He died for us so we could be with Him. Such pain for love. How could you doubt His love when He gave so much? Therefore we rejoice, not at the pain or loss, but at the love that was shown. And then we can be embraced in His loving arms."

Timothy put his cup down. He realized the extent of the truth that she spoke. The death of his little lamb was a mirror, a simple mirror reflection, compared to God giving up His Son, yet it was such a clear reminder of the terrible separation between God and him because of his sin. He knew it was there and he knew he couldn't hide it from God either. Even Tearle, who had barely known him, could point it out. He did not want to pretend it didn't exist, it was there and it had to be taken care of.

"God sent His Son here so many years ago. Many years ago he entered this city on a donkey. He was preparing the way for His Kingship; it took many years before He would take it over and live as it is now. He had to patiently wait for the right time to come so He could rule with justice.[242] Looking back on His sacrifice produces the greatest sense of worship. We are constantly reminded of Him who paid our redemption price.[243] The time is now, time to remember, time to worship. You have been fortunate to grow up in this era and experience His peace, goodness, and love."

"God is good." Timothy finally said, "Thank you for your words and the drink."

"You're welcome. That is why I am here, to serve,[244] to help, and to point people to Him. Wait, I have something for you, it is a piece of paper that may help you to keep your focus on God." She went over to a shelf and pulled a piece of paper from a book. It looked like the one he had read at Amos'. She handed him the paper.

"Thanks again, uh?"

"Louise, my name is Louise. I'm a resurrected saint, asked to see to the needs of travelers as they come to sacrifice."

"I knew Louise would be an excellent one to talk to, she has helped me before." Meyer stated.

"Louise, are you? Do you know Ross?"

"Yes, I know him well. We were married when we lived on earth together."

"Yes, I… he told me. I've always wanted to meet you." The three ended up talking for the rest of the day. Timothy was so glad that he could ask questions and hear stories about Louise's experience and how God had shown her love. His attention was captured and drawn to her as she spoke. Finally Meyer stood up and said it was time to go. They would come back into the city tomorrow and see other sacrifices and there was something else that he wanted to show Timothy.

Grateful that he didn't have to be alone, Timothy thanked Louise once again and followed Meyer out the door. He felt better. More confident, more secure in the fact that God loved him and that there was purpose in His plan.

Chapter 34

As they exited the city they heard the people singing.

> "And the ransomed of the Lord shall return,
> And come to Zion with singing,
> With everlasting joy on their heads.
> They shall obtain joy and gladness,
> And sorrow and sighing shall flee away."[245]

Timothy enjoyed the sounds around him, but kept quiet as he walked with Meyer. The two had not said one word by the time they reached Timothy's tent. Timothy hadn't realized the time had passed so quickly.

"I'll come look for you in the morning," Meyer stated as he turned and headed toward another section of the hill.

Timothy slipped inside his sukkot, alone, although he didn't feel completely alone. Once he was comfortably seated he unfolded the paper that Louise had given him. His eyes slowly read across the page.

> To Know God:
>
> - Listen to God's Word and receive it as the Holy Spirit interprets it, in application to oneself.
>   - Note God's nature and character, as His Word and works reveal it.
> - Accept His invitations and do what he commands.
>   - Recognize and rejoice in the love that He has shown in thus approaching you and drawing you into this divine fellowship.[246]

Timothy was amazed at the simplicity yet the truth that was revealed on the paper. He knew it was what he needed to follow. He knew this was the way to live his life. He started to plan that evening just how he was going to implement each step. He wanted to always be aware of God's Word and to follow His plan. He wanted to know God's character better than his own and match it. But most of all, he wanted to rejoice and be a part of the same fellowship that his family had had for as long as he could remember.

That night Timothy slept well, the paper that Louise had given him securely held in his hand.

Chapter 35

Meyer was at Timothy's tent long before he awoke. When Timothy finally stirred with the paper still clasped in his hand, he knew that they would be going somewhere. No words were needed. Timothy still had much on his mind. He knew the lamb had not slept with him last night, however, he had a feeling that there had been something there, a form of love and comfort, although not in either animal or human form.

That same feeling surrounded Timothy as the two silently walked toward the city. The hues of the rainbow still shone over the hills, the people still sang and brought their offerings to God. The sound still rose as if it lifted the mountain itself into the sky. All was the same as yesterday, but Timothy, he was not.

They made their way through the city, past the gate he entered yesterday to offer his sacrifice. Meyer made no mention of the other sacrifices or resurrected saints or people they passed by. His mind was focused on one thing, just what that one thing was, Timothy didn't know.

Quest for a True Heart

    Meyer took Timothy through another gate. There were a few people coming to and fro and a number of resurrected saints, their faces all aglow. They all seemed happy, so peaceful, so content and so loved. Just the sight of them calmed Timothy and gave his heart great peace.

    They approached a large building, the temple. The walls were high, the steps bare. Timothy wasn't sure that they should proceed, but Meyer didn't hesitate. He continued on, one step after another. When they finally reached the top Meyer stopped, with his hand on the door pushing to open it, he looked at Timothy, his eyes telling him to proceed.

    Timothy stood on the threshold. He hesitated for a moment, while looking in. He could see and feel a bright, warm light coming from within. He hesitantly took a step in then paused. Meyer nodded, encouraging him to continue. He took another step around the door.

    Timothy could see the floors were polished gold that sparkled like the sun and reflected the radiant light. The walls also glistened from the reflecting light. The place was glorious.[247] He was embraced by the light. There was no one else in the room. No other noise could be heard. All was still and silent as he stepped forward.

    There, before him sat the King of Kings, on His throne. This King did nothing to make Himself great. He wasn't parading around nor did He have His head up in a cocky fashion, thinking, "Hey everyone, look at me." He didn't have hundreds of servants surrounding Him running to and fro trying to see to His every need either. He just sat, humbly on His throne. His face was gentle, serene, and He had a loving smile on His lips. His presence filled the room. He was magnified. It wasn't that He was larger than the average person, He wasn't. At least, Timothy didn't think He was. It wasn't that His throne was the size of a room, coated in gold and jewels with bright lights to make Him look important. No, the light came from within Him,[248] brighter and purer than the sun. His character flowed out from Him, righteousness and faithfulness.[249] Timothy could feel the peace, love and joy flowing out from Him and cascading around the room and into the city. It was just as if you could reach out and touch it and take it for yourself.

The evidence was there, plain and easy to see on His hands, feet, and face. It was no longer just a story to Timothy. This man, this King, God, had suffered. The marks were not fake. The scars were deep, imbedded. They were the only dark spots on Him, spots that didn't radiate with brilliant light. They told the reality of His sacrifice.

As Timothy stood frozen, just past the doorway, taking in the sight of His King, he realized it wasn't fear that kept him frozen there. No, absolutely not fear. It was more like a sense of awe and gratefulness, one of thanksgiving and great humility that His God and King would not only give Him such blessings as his life and land, but would love him and allow him to come to the city where He reigned,[250] and not just that, but to sacrifice before Him and come into His presence.

Timothy had been so wrong, so off focus. How could he have wasted so much of his life and time on plants and gardening? How could he have thought anything was more important or deserved his attention more than God? How could he have missed all those opportunities to offer praise with his family or with those he met on his journey? And yet, even when he missed all those opportunities there sat the King, the Lord of Lords, the Mighty God, the Everlasting Father[251] willing and waiting for him to come, to love him and live for Him. He wasn't angry or upset. He wasn't preparing a lecture, nor was He disappointed in Timothy. He was only waiting to welcome him with open arms, waiting for him to step in and come forward.

How unworthy Timothy felt. He should be embarrassed, humiliated. He should not even consider going forward, but how could he not? He could not turn his back on this great God.

He could see the scars, even though the light was bright there was no mistaking the marks. He had indeed suffered. He knew, yet He was willing and still offered His love. It was incomprehensible. How? How could He?

An image of his little lamb slain and dead with blood dripping from its neck came to Timothy's mind. He could see the priest carry away its lifeless body. Those scars, those wounds, were the same as his lamb's. It had meant death for Him, death that should have been Timothy's.

Timothy did not make it all the way to His opened arms, but came crumpling down on the floor before the steps below His throne. Weeping and unable to look up he wanted God to know how truly sorry he was, that he was going to change, that he would from now on spend every moment of his life, every action, word and thought in effort to serve and please Him.

The LORD looked at Timothy as he bowed on the ground before Him and said, " 'My word be which goes forth from MY mouth; It will not return to Me empty, without accomplishing what I desire, And without succeeding in the matter for which I sent it.'[252] Therefore Timothy, you were sent here to learn of Me and change into a man whose whole heart is given in service to Me. As the rain which falls from the sky must water the earth, enabling the plants to grow, so My Word will fall onto you and will cause growth and change in you.[253] You have learned much on your journey, I am pleased with your heart[254] and your gift. Well done My servant, well done."[255]

"LORD God of Israel, *there is* no God in heaven or on earth like You, who keeps *Your* covenant and mercy with Your servants who walk before You with all their hearts,"[256] Timothy responded with tears streaming down his face.

As Timothy remained crumpled on the floor the King rose from His throne. Without pomp and circumstance, without a huge gathering or ceremony, He came down the steps, laid His scarred hands on Timothy's shoulders and lifted him up in His embrace.[257]

Love flowed from the King of Kings to His creation. All He wanted was to give Timothy love.[258] Timothy felt the love and acceptance. It flowed through him, coursing/surging through his body. It gave him hope. He knew from this point on life would be different.

He stood there elated. His heart rising with the tide of his emotions: joy, peace, hope, and love were spilling beyond the shores of himself. He now knew what was important. He would praise,[259] he would serve, he would love.

Sarah Stapley

> O Love that wilt not let me go,
> I rest my weary soul in thee;
> I give thee back the life I owe,
> That in thine ocean depths its flow
> May richer, fuller be.
>
> O light that followest all my way,
> I yield my flickering torch to thee;
> My heart restores its borrowed ray,
> That in thy sunshine's blaze its day
> May brighter, fairer be.[260]

Notes

[1] Philippians 3:14 Scripture taken from the NEW AMERICAN STANDARD BIBLE®, Copyright © 1960,1962,1963,1968,1971,1972,1973,1975,1977,1995 by The Lockman Foundation. Used by permission.
[2] Honoring God "Behind the Name" http://www.behindthename.com/name/timothy
[3] Leviticus 23:39
[4] Isaiah 54:5
[5] Luke 1:32
[6] II Chronicles 6:30
[7] Isaiah 66:10
[8] Revelation 19:11
[9] Ezekiel 34:25-29
[10] Isaiah 30:23
[11] Zech. 8:3
[12] Isaiah 65:20
[13] Isaiah 33:24
[14] Isaiah 65:20
[15] Jeremiah 3:17

[16] Ezekiel 34:28; Zechariah 14:11, *Scofield Study Bible NASB*, New York: Oxford University Press, 2005. p. 1745 note
[17] Psalm 72:2
[18] Zech. 14:7
[19] Isaiah 65:22
[20] Proverbs 25:21
[21] Ezekiel 34:14
[22] Ezekiel 43:2
[23] Isaiah 35:7
[24] Deuteronomy 33:13
[25] Zechariah 14:17
[26] Deuteronomy 11:13-15
[27] Numbers 29:13
[28] Isaiah 33:20
[29] Isaiah 2:3
[30] Exodus 20:12
[31] Monday
[32] Mark 6:9
[33] Isaiah 56:5-7; Zechariah 6:13
[34] Zechariah 14:16
[35] Psalm 48
[36] Mark 9:3
[37] Revelation 19:11-21
[38] Matthew 24:30
[39] Ezekiel 20:33-35; Jude 1:15; Revelation 19
[40] "nameberry", 2014. http://nameberry.com/babyname/Azrael
[41] Isaiah 4:3
[42] Land in Africa
[43] Desire to please
[44] Isaiah 65:21
[45] Isaiah 65:23
[46] Jeremiah 30:17
[47] Jeremiah 23:5; Ezekiel 34:22-23; Zechariah 14:9; I Corinthians 15:24-28
[48] Isaiah 42:4
[49] Zechariah 9:10
[50] Jeremiah 46:27
[51] Isaiah 25:8
[52] Isaiah 66:11-12
[53] Isaiah 11:9, 66:1; Ezekiel 38:23; Zechariah 2:10-11

54 Daniel 2:44, 4:3
55 Matthew 25:31-46; Malachi 4:6
56 Isaiah 1:26
57 Zechariah 14:16
58 Matthew19:14
59 Matthew 6:33
60 Jeremiah 23:4; I Corinthians 6:2; II Timothy 2:12; Revelation 2:26, 5:10, 20:4-6
61 Matthew 16:27; John 5:22; Revelation 22:12
62 II Corinthians 5:10
63 Matthew 4:26
64 Matthew 4:30
65 Matthew 5:12
66 Matt. 17:2
67 Daniel 12:3
68 Luke 11:36
69 Isaiah 60:14
70 Jeremiah 31:14
71 Isaiah 29:23
72 Joel 2:26
73 Jeremiah 3:15
74 Zechariah 14:17
75 John 20:19
76 Micah 4:3
77 Revelation 19
78 Revelation 19:14
79 Revelation 19
80 Romans 8:19-21
81 Psalm 23
82 Jeremiah 3:15; Jeremiah 23:4
83 I Peter 5:4
84 Isaiah 25:9
85 II Chronicles 19:9
86 Isaiah 35:1-2
87 Numbers 29:12
88 Mark 12:31
89 Psalm 72:7
90 Timothy 7:14
91 Walvoord, John F. *The Millennial Kingdom*. Grand Rapids, Michigan:

Zondervan, 1959. p. 309
[92] Mark 16:14
[93] Timothy 7:27
[94] Matthew 22:30
[95] Revelation 19:7
[96] I Corinthians 15:43
[97] John 3:6; Romans 8:29
[98] I Corinthians 15:52-53
[99] I Corinthians 15:44-45
[100] Revelation 21:9-22:5
[101] Isaiah 11:8, Micah 4:4
[102] Ezekiel 34:25
[103] Joel 2:28
[104] Isaiah 11:6, 65:25
[105] Isaiah 65:21-22
[106] Joel 2:24
[107] Deuteronomy 7:9
[108] Magnificent of faith – "Meaning of Names", 2014. http://www.meaning-of-names.com/african-names/bahaudeen.asp
[109] Exodus 11
[110] Jeremiah 31:34; Isaiah 11:9
[111] Psalm 4:8
[112] Psalm 84:5
[113] Psalm 115:15
[114] trouble - http://www.meaning-of-names.com/hebrew-names/jacan.asp
[115] Loyal, faithful - http://www.meaning-of-names.com/african-names/wafiyyah.asp
[116] "The Sacrifice of Worship, part 1 and 2" Dr. David Jeremiah (Nov. 5, 2013) http://www.oneplace.com/ministries/turning-point/listen/the-sacrifice-of-worship-part-1-375009.html
[117] Isaiah 2:11
[118] Grant, Robert. "O Worship the King", 1833.
[119] Lamentations 3:23
[120] Jeremiah 9:23-24
[121] Isaiah 48:17
[122] Psalm 139:1-10
[123] Suns rays light http://www.meaning-of-names.com/african-names/jamshid.asp
[124] Isaiah 65:18
[125] Stem http://www.meaning-of-names.com/english-names/tearle.asp

[126] Lemmel, Helen. "Turn your Eyes Upon Jesus", 1922.
[127] John 8:12
[128] I Samuel 15:22
[129] Luke 24:36
[130] Isaiah 25:9
[131] Jeremiah 31:34
[132] Ephesians 4:4; I Corinthians 12:14
[133] John 1:29
[134] Isaiah 50:6
[135] a temporary dwelling built during the Jewish holiday of Sukkot "About.com", 2014. http://judaism.about.com/od/glossary/g/sukkah.htm
[136] Leviticus 23:40
[137] Warren, Rick. *The Purpose Driven Life*. Grand Rapids, Michigan: Zondervan, 2002.
[138] Hebrews 13:5
[139] Romans 11:33
[140] Psalm 119:105
[141] Psalm 139:1-6
[142] Isaiah 35:3
[143] Packer, J.I. *Knowing God*. Illinois: Intervarsity Press, 1993. page 37
[144] Isaiah 12:1-6
[145] Isaiah 11:16
[146] Isaiah 2:3
[147] Zechariah 8:21
[148] Isaiah 11:1-2
[149] Isaiah 16:5
[150] Isaiah 12:3-4
[151] Shining http://www.meaning-of-names.com/jewish-names/meyer.asp
[152] Servant of God http://www.meaning-of-names.com/jewish-names/abdiel.asp
[153] II Corinthians 10:5
[154] Isaiah 26:3
[155] Psalm 34:8
[156] Deuteronomy 3:24
[157] Deuteronomy 6:4-6
[158] Psalm 95:1-5
[159] II Corinthians 4:6
[160] Isaiah 26:3
[161] Psalm 111:2
[162] Ezekiel 36:8

[163] Deuteronomy 11:9
[164] Joel 2:21
[165] Isaiah 11:11-12, 66:18-19,23
[166] Jeremiah 23:3
[167] Zechariah 8:21
[168] Romans 8:28
[169] The Sacrifice of Worship, part 1 and 2" Dr. David Jeremiah (Nov. 5, 2013)
[170] Hebrews 13:5
[171] Psalm 145:18
[172] Isaiah 61:7
[173] Isaiah 41:18-20
[174] Isaiah 35:6-10
[175] Ezekiel 47
[176] Isaiah 35:8
[177] Psalm 72
[178] Isaiah 2:2; Micah 4:1
[179] Luke 6:23; Romans 14:10, 12; Revelation 20:12
[180] II Corinthians 3:11-15
[181] Romans 14:12
[182] Revelation 3:11
[183] Deuteronomy 7:9
[184] Matthew 25:34; Mark 4:24-25; Luke 14:12-14; John 5:29; **I Corinthians 3:8**, 9:24-25; Ephesians 6:8; II Timothy 4:7-8; James 5:1; Revelation 11:18
[185] Proverbs 11:30
[186] I Thessalonians 2:19
[187] Matthew 6:1
[188] Luke 19:17
[189] Matthew 25:21
[190] I Peter 5:4
[191] II Timothy 4:8
[192] Revelation 1:16
[193] I Corinthians 3:13-15
[194] Revelation 2:10
[195] Psalm 150
[196] Luke 24:31
[197] Micah 4:1
[198] Isaiah 60:5
[199] Joel 2:26
[200] Psalm 135:1-6

[201] Psalm 136:1-3
[202] Psalm 135:21
[203] Revelation 21:11
[204] Isaiah 4:5
[205] Psalm 50:2
[206] John 12:13
[207] Zechariah 9:9
[208] Romans 8:19-21
[209] Amos 9:13
[210] Fairchild, Mary. "Feast of Tabernacles" About.com, 2014. http://christianity.about.com/od/biblefeastsandholidays/p/feastofbooths.htm
[211] Lemmel, Helen. "Turn Your Eyes upon Jesus." 1922. http://library.timelesstruths.org/music/Turn_Your_Eyes_upon_Jesus/
[212] Leviticus 23:35
[213] Psalm 95:1-7
[214] Jeremiah 30:19
[215] John 1:3
[216] Matthew 18:20
[217] Psalm 8:1
[218] II Corinthians 5:10
[219] Micah 4:2
[220] Psalm 96:8-10
[221] Dearman, Kirk. "We Bring the Sacrifice of Praise." Copyright © 1984 New Spring Publishing Inc. (ASCAP) (adm. at CapitolCMGPublishing.com) All rights reserved. Used by permission.
[222] Psalm 24:7-10
[223] Jeremiah 39:4
[224] Revelation 4:19-20
[225] Jeremiah 31:12
[226] Isaiah 60:14
[227] Jeremiah 31:13
[228] Isaiah 56:5-7
[229] Malachi 3:1-4
[230] Deuteronomy 6:4-7
[231] Isaiah 35:10
[232] Matthew 6:1; Ephesians 6:8; II Chronicles 6:30
[233] Isaiah 33:21
[234] Luke 8:16-18; 19: 24, 27; Matthew 24:28-29, 25:29; Mark 4:25
[235] Psalm 2:6; Daniel 2:35

[236] Numbers 29:12-16
[237] Jeremiah 33:18; Ezekiel 44:15-16; Malachi 3:3-4
[238] I Kings 2:3
[239] Isaiah 56:7
[240] II Chronicles 30:18-19
[241] Watts, Isaac. "When I Survey the Wondrous Cross" http://library.timelesstruths.org/music/When_I_Survey_the_Wondrous_Cross/, 1707
[242] Psalm 96:13; Isaiah 9:7, 35:1; John 5:30
[243] *The Millennial Kingdom* p. 312
[244] Galatians 5:13
[245] Isaiah 35:10
[246] J.I. Packer, *Knowing God.* page 37
[247] Isaiah 11:10
[248] Hebrews 1:3; Isaiah 2:19; Isaiah 40:4-5; Isaiah 18:4; Isaiah 62:2
[249] Isaiah 11:5
[250] Jeremiah 16:21
[251] Isaiah 9:6-7
[252] Isaiah 55:11
[253] Isaiah 55:10
[254] II Chronicles 6:30
[255] Matthew 25:21
[256] II Chronicles 6:14
[257] Isaiah 2:17; Isaiah 11:3-4
[258] Isaiah 66:13
[259] Isaiah 56:7; Isaiah 61:3
[260] Matheson, George. "O Love that will not Let me Go." 1882. Cyber Hymnal. http://www.cyberhymnal.org/htm/o/l/oltwnlmg.htm

RELIGIOUS FICTION

The great Deceiver is bound and the true King sits on the throne. In a world of near perfection, how can anything go wrong? Is life pure joy and delight or is it rules and regulations in submission to the King?

Timothy has been entrusted to represent his family at the Feast of Tabernacles. There is no alternative—he must go—however, if he does not offer his sacrifice with a pure heart, his family will suffer the same dire consequences as those who don't send a representative. Will Timothy be able to offer his sacrifice appropriately or will his family suffer?

As life unfolds for Timothy, Ross and other resurrected saints recall their previous lives on earth and the rewards they received from the King. Serving with Him in the Millennium has been an unbelievable blessing. Their job now is to guide Timothy on his journey. Will they make a difference? Will they be able to accomplish the task God has entrusted in their care? Can they show Timothy what true worship really is?

Join Timothy on his journey to Jerusalem in a *Quest for a True Heart*.

Sarah Stapley has a bachelor's degree in biblical studies, elementary education and a master's degree in education. In 2012, she completed a fiction writing course. Raised in a godly family, her parents always encouraged her and her two siblings to become more Christlike and share Christ's love with others. Born and raised in Canada, Sarah now makes her home between the United States and the Bahamas, where she hopes to impact the next generation for Christ.

WestBow Press
A DIVISION OF THOMAS NELSON & ZONDERVAN

CPSIA information can be obtained
at www.ICGtesting.com
Printed in the USA
FFOW02n1057281014
8386FF